THE ABBEY OF EVOLAYNE

THE ABBEY OF EVOLAYNE

BY PAULE RÉGNIER

TRANSLATED FROM THE FRENCH
BY SAMUEL SLOAN

HARCOURT, BRACE AND COMPANY

NEW YORK

843.9
R342a

Typography by Robert Josephy

PRINTED IN THE UNITED STATES OF AMERICA
BY QUINN & BODEN COMPANY, INC., RAHWAY, N. J.

26145

To Louis Buzzini

PART ONE

I. NO person who has received the gift of happiness, however jealously he watches over his treasure, is conscious of the exact moment he begins to let it slip through his fingers. As day fades into night, summer into winter, so joy insensibly changes to sorrow, abundance to want. It is only later, when one's grief is fixed and permanent, that the soul in its destitution looks back upon the past and then can recognize the first shadows that fell upon its destiny, and the hour which marked the beginning of its downfall. All the ordinary incidents and events of daily life, every choice one makes between this action or that, seem at the time to be of no lasting consequence.

Thus, when in the course of a trip, Adélaide Adrian first heard the name "Evolayne," she felt no twinge of apprehension. It was simply the name of a strange place that she was curious to visit. Nothing warned her that at all cost she should avoid it.

She had succeeded in persuading her husband to take a long vacation that summer. Michel Adrian was worn out both by the exactions of his profession as surgeon and by the strenuous social life which they led, and it was only after prolonged urging that he had consented to leave his practice to an assistant for three months and to set off on a motor trip with his wife.

They departed with no definite destination in mind. The Ardennes attracted Michel, for he had been through them at the beginning of the war, and he liked the idea of revisiting the valley of the Meuse with his wife.

"We will find some nice little place around there where we can settle down for a long rest," he told her. But that rough, desolate region offered few inducements to motorists. The inns were scarce and ill-equipped. And though he was an extremely active man and liked outdoor life, Michel could not habituate himself to long periods of leisure. At Joigny-sur-Meuse, at Layfour, at Monthermé, he declared:

"Here's just the place." And in two days, tramping from morning till night, he had exhausted all its charms. Then he wanted to set out again, avid for something new.

"I don't call this resting, I call it getting ourselves all the more tired," said Adélaide.

And she followed him, a little wearily, but none the less indulgent. She knew that, with his ceaseless eagerness to add to his knowledge, one place, one book, could never suffice him. She admired that insatiability of mind in him; to it, in the intellectual realm, she owed an immense debt. Their rôles in life were very different. To him belonged the task of

4

seeking out, to her that of guarding the treasure acquired. Michel discovered for her many beautiful things in books, in art, in nature, which would have escaped her. He seized them, played his enthusiasm over them, then passed on, while she, slow to understand, slow to open her heart, cherished them and savored their loveliness long afterward.

One morning they reached the town of Givet on the flat stony plain near the Belgian border. Neither had any desire to stop there; so, as soon as they had finished luncheon, they scanned the maps for some further destination. Adélaide wanted to turn back, for she preferred the places she knew and country that was familiar. Michel suggested going on into Belgium.

"Beyond the frontier," he said, "it turns beautiful again. We could follow the valley of the Meuse as far as Dinant, or even as far as Namur."

"As far as the sea," she sighed. "That's the only thing that will stop you."

He smiled lightly, looking at her, and straightway she was ready to do whatever he wished. He had a strong, commanding face at once care-worn and young. Deep lines furrowed his forehead and his cheeks. His eyes, from constant watching over illness, always had an expression of seriousness and pity, no matter what the circumstances. But his smile, radiant and tender, transfigured his countenance, lending it an almost feminine charm. For a moment, it hovered

5

on his lips, then he again bent over the map spread out upon the table.

"Well, let's find something nearer."

His wandering finger halted on a spot which seeemed to catch his interest.

"Evolayne," he exclaimed. "Are we that close? The abbey of Evolayne."

The name awakened some distant memory in Adélaide, but she could not identify it.

"What is it?" she asked. "Some old ruin or an abandoned abbey?"

"By no means. It's a modern Benedictine monastery founded less than sixty years ago. Don't you remember? That's the cloister in which Henri Darbaud has immured himself, the man who was such a dear friend of mine in our student days. He's called Dom Athanase now."

Among all the letters of congratulation which they had received when they were married, the one that was most striking suddenly flashed into Adélaide's mind. It had been written upon a sheet of paper at the top of which was a cross and the single word "Pax," and its tone had been a mixture of gayety and austerity. One sentence came back to her, in which the monk had blessed them and wished them many children. The memory of it made her blush. After seven years of married life she had lost all hope of having children. She was sorrier for her husband than for herself. She often had the impression that she was not wholly sufficient to him, and that children would have bridged the void that she sensed between them. Covertly, her eyes rested for a moment on Michel. Would she ever wholly understand what was in his heart? At the same time she replied, with a note of banter in her voice:

"Dom Athanase! Good heavens, how do you happen to be remembering him affectionately after all this time? I thought you had rather lost track of him."

Michel acknowledged his guilt. What with putting things off, and not having time, he scarcely ever wrote letters and he had let the monk's last epistle go several years without reply. But he maintained that their friendship had not suffered on that account. He would make up for his neglect by going to surprise the priest in his monastery. There would surely be an inn near the abbey where they could stop. Adélaide, bethinking herself that the presence of a friend might perhaps hold Michel in one spot for a little time, agreed eagerly:

"Then by all means, on to Evolayne!"

For some minutes longer Michel studied the map, tracing out the shortest route, calculating the number of kilometers. By pressing along fast they might be in Evolayne for dinner. As soon as they had crossed the border, he set off at a furious rate, slowing down only for villages. Adélaide did not relish their whirlwind progress. Numbed by the speed and

7

the noise and the dust, she kept her eyes on the map spread out on her lap, and that fixed point where they would finally stop. Toward six o'clock she announced:

"We're nearly there!"

Shortly after, on a distant hill, they saw the towers of the abbey, then the abbey itself. Michel stopped the car. The silence of the fields, following the noise of the motor, seemed godlike. On either side of the road their eyes were refreshed by the sight of meadows as green and lustrous as the grass of a formal garden. A brook flowed close by and they could hear its soft murmuring. The smiling landscape swept gradually up to the horizon in a succession of fertile valleys and wooded slopes. And crowning everything stood the abbey. As far as they could see, all lines converged upon it. The late afternoon sunlight shattered on its gray mass and lay about it in a sort of golden haze, shot with sparks. The abbey, unlike most churches, was not a part of a village or group of houses. About its feet lay only trees and fields and pastures with a few scattered animals, seeming to submit contentedly to its peaceful domination. For a long time Michel gazed at it in silence.

"It's far more beautiful, its being alone like that," he said finally. "It isn't that the country is so majestic, but the abbey seems to lend it a soul. In the midst of all this quiet, it's a symbol of both man and God."

"And for parishioners, it has the birds," went on

Adélaide, falling under the spell. "It's the parish-church of butterflies and bees and woods and hills: Our Lady of the Solitudes!"

They started on again. From time to time, a turn in the road or some quirk of the landscape hid the abbey from view. Then they looked for it and as soon as it came into sight pointed it out to each other with a look or a gesture. They stopped at the foot of the hill which carried it on its brow. There, in the valley, near the station of Evolayne, set about by fields, stood a picturesque little inn: the *Hôtellerie de la Drachme Perdue*. Adélaide clapped her hands.

"It's perfect! Everything around here is biblical. It makes one want to eat the mess of pottage that Esau coveted, and drink the wine of the wedding feast of Cana. See, down there is the well to which the Samaritan woman went, and Job's dunghill beyond it."

Without difficulty they secured two pleasant, airy rooms. A crucifix and a piece of blessed palm over each bed distinguished this inn from all the others in which they had stopped. They had come to a sort of Holy Land, where travelers were transformed into pilgrims. Outside their windows, beyond the road and railway which paralleled the brook, stretched a broad meadow with the abbey crowning the hill above it.

"We will be able to see it as much as we like, from the moment we wake up!" cried Michel.

9

"I really believe you're falling in love with it!" teased Adélaide.

They dined on a terrace in the open air, and they constantly lifted their eyes to the great mass of stone which was throwing its shadow down the valley. To highly cultured people such as they, tired of the ostentation of the modern world, the combination, which religion offers, of the archaic with the living and the timeless, suddenly gripped their imaginations. They had read Huysmans. They knew through him of the grandeur of the Benedictine Order, the Order which has never cast an anathema upon earthly beauty, whose aim it is to honor God by the liturgy, ceremonies, and ancient rites which it alone, resisting the spiritless innovations so common in parish churches, has preserved in all their purity. Such a conception of the religious life pleased Michel as it did Adélaide. They looked forward to attending the solemn ceremonies, not from idle curiosity, but from profound and reverent interest. Though they were not believers, they had sufficient breadth of mind to admire the monks there above them, who from morning to evening, from youth to old age, had no other occupation, no other duty than to sing the praises of God. For such an attitude to be taken by man, indifferent to the things of earth, rapt in unceasing communication with the eternal, seemed singularly noble to them.

It was still daylight when they finished their dinner, and Michel asked if the abbey was still open. He was told that it was, and that a last office, compline, took place at half past eight.

"Would you like to go, Adé, or are you too tired?" he asked.

"Not at all, the walk would do me good."

A winding path led up to the abbey. It was bordered on the left by the woods, on the right by low bushes and thickets which gave intermittent glimpses of the valley and the green fields below, cut into parcels by hedges and thin rows of trees. The brook was hidden between its narrow banks but one could trace its course from the blue mist which hovered along its edges and wound with it through the meadows.

Sensuously, Adélaide drank in the nature about her, breathing deep of every fleeting perfume, listening to the calls and the silence of the country. She opened her arms to the evening breeze. She snatched up handfuls of grass and leaves and bark, squeezing them in her hands to capture the smell of the soil and the meadows and the woods. While she was frolicking, Michel moved along with his even stride, absorbed in his memories. Guessing his thoughts, she fell in with him and said:

"Tell me about Father Athanase."

"O," he said, "we were strange friends. We never agreed about anything and we were always arguing. Our debates used to go on and on interminably, and

when we weren't wrangling we'd be spending our
time thinking up arguments against each other. Darbaud's thoughts were only of God. I had no use for
anything but science. I was certain it could make
earth a paradise. The war proved how wrong I was
in that. It knocked to pieces all the pretty conception of progress that I had been building up."

He sighed and then went on.

"Just the same, it's good to have had high ideals
when you were young. Darbaud's weren't of this
world, but I respected them as he respected mine.
That's why we liked each other. I owe a great deal
to him. His intelligence was quick and subtle, somewhat dogmatic, but it made me discipline my own
tendency to jump at conclusions. He made me live
for ideas only, at an age when passions might have
dragged us down so low. Even at that age, he was certain of his vocation, and he used to talk to us like a
young priest. There was a sort of innocence and
purity about him that made him dominate us and
kept us from teasing him. But there was nothing intolerant about him. He didn't pass judgment or try
to lecture us. He was content to be an example and
to say 'no' when we wanted to take him to some bad
place or make him read a bad book. Temptations
had no attraction for him. Everything that was im-
moral simply bored him. How surprised he was when
we told him about our first love affairs. You should
have heard him talk about women, and throw his

arms up in the air and say: 'What place have those bundles of fluff in an intelligent man's life?' "

Adélaide was amused by the remark at first, then it piqued her, as if Michel in repeating it had associated himself with the monk's views.

"What place do we have in your lives, after all?" she sighed.

He shrugged his shoulders. He was accustomed to her continual doubting of his love for her.

"You are right," he said, with the tender irony that he used sometimes when she talked that way, "I have never been able to understand how I could have been so harebrained as to tie my happiness up in you."

They stopped and gazed at each other. She was standing a few feet from him, her head and shoulders bent a little to one side and her white skirt molding her form. Shafts of rose and golden evening light shone about her, seeming to skip lightly over the inanimate objects so that they might concentrate on her body so full of life. The sun and the shadows playing on her arms and bare neck, flecked her skin. Her face had none of that sharp, angular, almost harsh beauty which framed by bobbed hair was regarded as the height of feminine attractiveness after the war. Her unusually soft, jet black hair was waved gently about her cheeks, pale as pearls. Her features were small, the chin delicate and a little pointed. Her eyes, set above prominent cheek bones, were dark and lustrous as water flowing in the shad-

13

ows of a steep bank. Two fine lines starting from her
nostrils, circled her mouth, emphasizing its beauty. At
that hour, when the dark pupils were growing darker
still, when her thoughts could no longer be mirrored
there, all the expression in her face centered in her
mouth. Ever mobile, it was curving now in a hesitant,
sadly sweet smile. Her lips parted imperceptibly, imploring him.

When he spoke, Michel's voice was uncertain.

"Don't be so beautiful!"

Why, knowing that she belonged to him utterly,
was there that expression of sadness and renunciation
in his face? Why did their tenderest moments always
seem so precarious to both of them? A dull, familiar
grief gripped Adélaide's heart, and she forced herself
to laugh.

"Am I so beautiful that you can't bear to look at
me?"

Playfully she raised her arms and stretched her
black tulle scarf before her white face and her shining eyes. Thus veiled, she moved close to Michel and
he, joining in her fancy, kissed her softly on the lips
through the thin material. In the blue eyes close to
hers she saw love quicken, then slowly ebb. The kiss
was light, but they had never given one exactly like
it. The exquisite moment hovered an instant on the
perishable heights of happiness, then faded into the
past. Already the red of the setting sun was dulling,
already Michel's heart was less stirred, already she

felt less beautiful and less beloved. She turned aside, caught sight of some flowers beside the path, called out joyfully:

"There's some sweet clover!"

She loved that modest bloom, with its sweet, persistent odor. She made a bouquet of it as they climbed along the path, which, finally, with a sharp turn brought them out before the abbey.

There was nothing in its architecture, spiritless pseudo-Gothic, which could have stirred an artist. It owed its beauty to its solitariness. A wood flanked it on the left. A great esplanade lay before it, and on the right, its outbuildings stretched off along the road which skirted the top of the hill. No wall surrounded it. Accessible to everyone, it held out its welcome to pilgrim and traveler, and, dominating the peaceful countryside, thrusting its towers to the heavens as a sign, seemed to call to those passing far below in the valley. The drapery of the clouds formed an ever-changing back-drop for the mass of stone. Now that the sun no longer played on them, they were turning soft-hued, blue, and ghostly. In the court, a few monks were pacing up and down. With their crown-like tonsures, their long scapulars, their leather cinctures, they looked like silhouettes stepped from the past. The world they reincarnated was so strange that Adélaide, entering it unexpectedly, felt suddenly embarrassed to be a woman and clothed in white. She drew her dark cape about her. Michel had halted, as had she. Suddenly he started, pointing to a monk who was standing near a pile of freshly cut branches, talking to a lay brother. The latter's head was bent respectfully before him.

"If memory doesn't deceive me," he whispered, "I think that's he—Darbaud—Father Athanase."

"You had better inquire," murmured Adélaide in a hushed voice, for she did not want to break the embracing silence.

While she stayed behind, Michel went on. She saw him, pretending to wander aimlessly about, draw nearer to the monk, scrutinize him, then suddenly with an exclamation they recognized each other and hurried to meet. After the first enthusiastic greetings they came toward Adélaide, deep in conversation. From the distance, she studied the monk curiously. He was a man of medium height. His face was in the shadow, but she could make out his sharp features and noticed that his hair was so thin that his tonsure was scarcely visible at all. When he wasn't talking or smiling he held his lips pressed tight together, in a voluntary grimace, as if they were closed forever by a vow of silence.

Michel came up to his wife and presented her to his friend.

"Let me introduce to you," he said. . . .

But Adélaide, either from mischievousness or spite, cut him short, and finished for him:

". . . A little bundle of fluff."

The monk looked stupefied. Michel, in thorough embarrassment, explained to him that those had once been his own words. At that, Dom Athanase burst into a laugh, and the man of the world appearing beneath the priest, he turned to Adélaide:

"Ah, Madame," he said, "that is treason on the part of a friend whom I trusted. You can see how golden is silence when of all the more or less weighty opinions which I used to expound in Michel's presence, this rather uncharitable one is the only one that he remembers. I hope that you are not going to judge me by a schoolboy's intemperate jest."

His cordial frankness won Adélaide. In her turn she was excusing herself lightly for so ungracious a remark, when the monk raised his eyes and looked at her. She broke off, disconcerted, in the middle of a sentence. His glance pierced through her, blinding as a flash of light, then turned away. She knew that in that one glance she had been revealed to him more fully than she could have revealed herself to anyone. But he allowed no inkling of what he thought to show on his face.

"How long are you planning to stay?" he asked.

Adélaide felt the tension relax within her.

"As for that, Father, I am counting on you to keep Michel here a while. His health rather worries me. For two weeks, under the excuse of taking a rest, we have been on the go constantly. We haven't stayed three days in the same place and I'm in terror for fear he will be wanting to start off again day after tomorrow."

"I know how we can put a stop to that," said the priest. "I shall do him the honors of the abbey. Rest assured, it is not so easy to leave it."

As he spoke of the abbey, an expression of tender pride softened the sternness of his face. His eyes shone like the unwavering flames in a hearth which no winds can reach. One could see in them how full and abiding was the fire of his faith.

"No," he went on softly, almost caressingly, "I have seen strangers come to Evolayne quite by chance and stay here for months. Are you going to attend compline?"

They replied that they were. A moment after, a slow sonorous tolling announced the approaching hour of office. The monk bowed to Adélaide and pressed Michel's hand.

"Until tomorrow then, old friend. I shall wait for you at eight o'clock, after my Mass. Don't think any more about leaving. The health of the body depends largely on that of the soul, and here you will find peace."

Michel and Adélaide entered the abbey. The pulsating silence of the fields gave way suddenly to a silence that was stunning and absolute: the silence of death or of prayer. The fading day cast only a pale, gray light into the nave, rendering more solemn its forest of pillars, more mysterious its vaulting arches. The altar, in the depths of the choir far from the congregation, was scarcely discernible. Some pilgrims, men and women, were waiting in perfect stillness for the office. Motionless. They were like inert forms whom their souls had abandoned. The two newcomers, kneeling like them, imitated their immobility. It did not seem constraining to them. Michel, the man who could not tolerate inaction, who always had to have conversation, or a book, or a problem, or a discovery to keep him in one place, Michel knelt relaxed, meditative, patient in the shadows. After a little time, vague, almost imperceptible silhouettes began to move about. The monks were coming in one by one at random, gliding softly over the flagstones, finding their places in the stalls.

Night had now completely fallen. A single lamp shone feebly in the middle of the choir over the lectern. Standing there, a priest read a few prayers, then, all together, the monks began the *Confiteor*. They stood in two long rows, their heads bowed low, and struck their breasts, each gesture in perfect unison. The prayer finished, they sat down in their stalls for the recitation of the psalms.

Adélaide had been brought up in a convent and she had heard them many times. The murmur of the voices scanning the verses of a dead language did not seem monotonous to her. She knew their meaning. Forgotten phrases came back to her memory:

The things you say in your hearts, be sorry for

them upon your beds. . . . Many say, who showeth
us good things. . . . Let dreams depart, night's phan-
toms fly, lest they become our virtue's test; curb
Thou our raging enemy, that we in chaste repose
may rest. . . .

In days gone by she had often repeated these
phrases distractedly, but here in this setting and in
the dimness, they seemed to assume a new significance, and force, and gravity.

On weekdays, the office was simply recited. Only
the *Salve Regina* was chanted. For the Lord, words
alone, severe unadorned praise, could suffice, but for
the Virgin, for the Mother, softer accents were
needed, a winged prayer swept aloft by music. A
great wave of sound swept through the nave as the
monks rose in a body. Their voices, supported lightly
by the organ's soft accompaniment, rose to the arches
in a swelling chorus like the cry of a single soul.
Joyfully they called upon their queen. They might
tremble before the Father, even before Him who was
crucified, but before her, so accessible, so pitying,
girt with all earthly charms, they were free, confident,
joyful. They besought her fearlessly, with a child's
loving boldness. They lingered tenderly over the last
invocations and the name Mary died upon their lips
in slow, caressing modulations.

Then, for a long moment, silence reigned in the
shadowy church. The souls of the priests which had
been as if welded into one, broke once more into sep-

arate entities. Each one continued his own prayer in secret, returned to his own meditation.

A signal brought the dark, kneeling forms to their feet. Two by two, the monks filed down from the choir, the Father Abbot, recognizable by the great silver cross which hung from about his neck, at their head. Behind them followed the lay brothers. These wore no scapulars, their robes clasped simply by the leather cinctures. Nearly all were bearded, and their faces were at once strong and gentle. Their big hands, hardened by the work in the fields, were clasped together in a clumsy, touching gesture. At the foot of the steps, each one paused a moment on the left before the altar of Saint Benedict where candles were burning. A short prayer, then the long procession closed up once more behind the Father Abbot and disappeared through the door of the cloister.

A few of the monks, however, did not follow the others. They lingered here and there on their knees before their favorite side altars, while the brother porter who was waiting to close the abbey jangled his keys and gave the visitors a nod to depart. Adélaide touched Michel on the shoulder. His behavior surprised her a little. For while she had followed the service, imitating the gestures of the monks, getting up and seating herself as they did, Michel had remained the entire time on his knees, his head in his hands. For a moment she thought he was asleep, but she did not need to repeat her gentle warning. He crossed himself, then rose and followed her.

Outside, their mood persisted. They walked down the path wordlessly. Though the stars were out, the night was dark. They could not see each other's faces. Adélaide first broke the silence.

"It was beautiful," she sighed.

"I understand now," said Michel pensively, "what Darbaud's life has been, what it still is. What does it matter if the war has destroyed millions of men—death doesn't exist for him. What does it matter if this world is shaken—he has no place in it. His place is in the serene and in the eternal. He has no need of explanations. It is enough for him to stand before God, to commune with Him ceaselessly, to implore Him and to give thanks. As you say, it is very beautiful."

"Michel," asked Adélaide, "you prayed, didn't you?"

"Yes," he answered in a low voice. "How could one help it?"

"I too," she said happily. "It's very easy to understand why. One can't help sharing in anything which is really great. When I am in a foreign city and see a regiment go by with a flag, I bow my head in respect even though it is not my own country that I am honoring. In the same way, in the presence of those monks whose faith I admire even though I don't share it, I join in their prayers. There is nothing hypocritical in that."

"Certainly not," murmured Michel, after a moment's hesitation.

She was content to have been able to explain their common attitude. At the hour when they were beginning to be so profoundly divided, she rejoiced once more in their perfect harmony. She had dropped into the position she loved at Michel's side. Her head resting on his shoulder, his arm about her waist, she let herself be carried along by the rhythm of his step. She surrendered herself dreamily, happily. She had no other life but his. It seemed to her as if she might be another Eve, just drawn from this man's side, so wholly was she like him, his second self, his image. And she did not imagine that he could have a single dream, a single aspiration that was not in her.

II. MICHEL did not tire of Evolayne as he had of other places. He talked no more of pressing on. The cloister of the abbey, closed to women, was open in part to men. The library, rich and well-stocked, became his favorite retreat. He spent hours there, talking frequently with Father Athanase. Adélaide did not see a great deal of her husband, but she did not complain. She was not one of those women who are so jealously in love that they do not wish to allow the man whom they have chosen for master and slave to have more liberty than they demand for themselves. Bound up in Michel as she was, her own strong personality kept alive her taste for independence and for being by herself. His presence was not indispensable to her. She was glad to be away from him sometimes, realizing how damaging it is for love to become a habit and how much the intimacies of daily life take away from individuality. Being separated from him, she understood him better, saw him once more at his true worth.

Moreover she needed to be alone occasionally to reopen the book of her own life and re-read it page by page, trying to seize the significance of each event, and so by the past to understand the present and try to foresee the future. To this examination of hers and Michel's hearts she brought all her faculties, for it was not an easy task. Smooth-flowing as was their life together, there was some mysterious factor in it, some reason which she could not explain why their great happiness seemed so lacking in security.

Perhaps she had waited for happiness too long, and had too long doubted whether she might ever attain it. She had never known it as a child in the convent to which she had been sent at seven after her mother's death. She had been ill-adapted to her surroundings there, and had grown up without any friends among her companions, creating imaginary joys for herself since she had no others, escaping from monotonous reality into a fanciful world which was continually falling in ruins and being built up again. Nor had she known happiness later in her father's house, where she had had to submit to the domination of a narrowly religious and strait-laced step-mother who undertook to suppress all her young enthusiasms as being against religious or social rules. In the desperation of her loneliness, all her unfathomable aspirations toward happiness changed into one fierce, devouring desire: the desire for love.

When she was twenty-three, her father died and she escaped from the provinces to come to live with her brother, ten years her senior, who was practicing medicine in Paris. It was there that she met Michel.

From the very beginning, he interested her more than any other of Maurice Verdon's friends. Not because of his brilliance in his profession, which she heard being praised constantly by all about her, but because that brilliance went hand in hand with other qualities which in her eyes were still more important: strength of character and sensitiveness and a desire for higher things than wealth and reputation. She did not like people who lived aimlessly and listlessly. Among all the young doctors who came to her brother's house, Michel Adrian alone seemed to feel that he had a calling; he alone took the duties seriously which the others fulfilled conscientiously but without attaching great importance to them. Nevertheless she could not understand him completely. He listened and observed more than he revealed himself, and his changes of mood disconcerted her. Though he had been a constant visitor since she had established herself at her brother's, he disappeared sometimes, unaccountably, for weeks at a time. One day she reproached him good-humoredly for one of his absences.

"I go through crises at times when I feel that I have to hide myself away," he explained simply. "Whenever I take care of someone who is hopelessly ill and have to watch their last agonies without being able to do anything for them, it's torture for me. Wherever I go, I think of that person suffering and

26

dying, and I can't forget it. I can't see anybody then. Why should I sadden others?"

She felt a great surge of tenderness for him:

"I understand so well!" she exclaimed. "I would feel the same way in your place. . . . I've always been amazed to hear my brother and his friends say that they forget their patients as soon as they have left them."

"Yes," murmured Michel, "they have almost all been granted that blessing, but not I. To tell the truth, I don't believe many people see suffering. But even when I was a child I was aware of it everywhere and it made me desolate. I have never, never, been able to accustom myself to it."

"But how, if you feel that way," asked Adélaïde, touched by his confession, "can you have chosen a profession in which there is so much suffering?"

He laughed gently, mocking himself:

"I suppose I hoped I could cure everybody."

She realized then how exacting of himself he was, and at the same time how inevitably his powers must fall short of his hopes; how much he suffered before the reality which he could not change. From then on she not only admired Michel, she felt pity for him. And from those two emotions love was already being born. He, feeling himself understood, opened his heart more and more to her. She knew what he was attempting for his patients. She shared his anxieties, triumphed with him, consoled him in his failures.

27

As their friendship grew, they fell into the habit of going to concerts and to the theater together, of reading the same books. They found that their reactions were usually the same. Michel's intelligence was not cold, as masculine intelligence so often proves to be. He had more than a superficial curiosity about beauty. It moved him simultaneously in his mind and his heart and in all his being. Like Adélaide, he too found satisfaction in seeing, through the medium of a work of art, how life itself could take on greater horizons, the hidden essences of things become manifest. They felt the same thrill of ecstasy at lifting the veil of Isis. Michel, with his wider culture, urged Adélaide to the effort which alone permits the appreciation of the highest works of art. She followed him with enthusiasm on the dizzy paths along which he led her. She read for him, thinking only that she might please him. Their mutual understanding became daily more perfect, and seeing that their minds and their hearts were as one, they decided to join their two lives forever.

Nothing was lacking in their happiness, not even the overflowing of it which brings suffering. They were married July 27, 1914, and they loved each other in a world on the brink of disaster. They were united to one another with anguish in their hearts at the thought of the separation, perhaps eternal, which was to come. Michel was mobilized in the

Medical Corps, and took leave of his bride on the 4th of August.

Then days of waiting began again for Adélaide. No longer, as it had been in her girlhood, a vague waiting for some hazily imagined joy, but a waiting for a definite happiness, the waiting for a single person whom death was threatening night and day. He came back several times on hasty furloughs, but she found him only to lose him again, and she wept for him even while she still held him in her embrace.

When peace gave them back to each other, anxiety had become habitual to Adélaide. It made her love all the greater, for, believing it was constantly in danger, it abated none of its intensity. Perhaps she might have admitted to herself the disillusionment which every person feels on attaining the object of his desires, if something had not warned her that Michel was experiencing a greater disillusionment than she. She knew that no other woman meant anything to him. Despite the storms which frequently resulted from the clash of their too similar, strong-willed natures, there was a perfect friendship between them, a deep concord of tastes and thought. Whatever the intangible thing was that sometimes seemed to raise a barrier between them, she told herself it could only be the result of the difference in their ages, accentuated by the four years of the war which for Michel counted doubly. Of what those years had done to him he never spoke, he could not speak. His wife had no way of understanding that past which held him prisoner. Having feared for one person only, and that one being now restored to her, she could forget the anguish she had known. At thirty, she was beginning to live again, but he, who had shared the dying agonies of so many men, had been seared in his soul beyond recovery. Nothing held the same savor for him as for his young wife.

He was at pains, however, not to prevent her from enjoying the pleasures to which she had a right. He went out with her frequently though he could only feel an immense disgust at the frivolousness and vanity of social life.

"These people are so shallow, so boring," he would sometimes say. "Always the same little intrigues, the same petty ambitions and pointless excitements. The war has taught them nothing."

Then he would add, turning his bitterness on himself:

"But what right have I to criticize them? Are we any better? We are always going to exhibits and concerts and theaters just as those idlers do."

Adélaide protested. There was at least some conscious aim in her and Michel's lives which differentiated them from the merely worldly, however similar they might seem on the surface.

"Where they are looking for nothing except to be amused," she explained, "we are looking for something spiritual, for something which will stir us and deepen our capacity for love. Beauty is rare indeed, and I'll admit what we find is counterfeit often as not, but nevertheless we do find it sometimes, and it is something so important to us that we would be ready to die for it."

He parried, half convinced:

"But one doesn't die for a beautiful line of poetry, or a phrase in music, or a picture, or a statue. Beauty demands no real sacrifice of us."

"Who knows?" she said. "It's you who taught me that by always striving after the highest things, by never ceasing to reach after beauty, one contributed in one's own small way to making the world purer, to keeping its grandeur uppermost. Art nourishes a spirit of heroism in us that makes us ready to do whatever may be required of us."

He listened to her repeating his own words; once more he felt their force, yet he was not wholly satisfied:

"Yes, but what is required of us?"

"For me, it's very simple," she said, with touching confidence. "It is to please you, to give you as perfect love as I can. And for you, isn't it enough of a task to ease human suffering?"

"I'm paid for that!" he protested quickly.

"But you take care of the poor too, without asking them anything for it. You help them, you give them your pity. So many people depend on you."

One day he confessed:

"I don't know why, but I feel ashamed that we are so happy."

She told him that he was an ascetic who had missed his calling, a pagan mystic. She thought that the moral tension of the four years at the front, when as a matter of duty he had had to be ready for every self-sacrifice, still persisted in him. It was from then that he had taken this desire to outstrip himself, this thirst for renunciation.

"Very well," she suggested, "let's go away, let's have no more to do with the social life. Become a country doctor. You can devote yourself entirely to the poor and I will take care of them with you. We will have a little house with a thatched roof and I will dress in homespun if you like. And I won't cut my hair because that's not a sacrifice any more, but the height of style. I will let it hang in two braids and I will go barefoot."

He laughed when she talked that way. But he continued to be troubled and she was conscious of it always.

What did it all mean? Why, when they were so richly blessed, should there be these discordant notes of discontent and foreboding in their song of happiness? Why had Michel had that expression of farewell in his face as he looked at her the evening of their arrival in Evolayne? Reflecting upon it now, she felt touched and happy that Michel had suddenly, and without reason, been shaken at the thought of losing her. Ordinarily it was she who felt the fear, he who was satiated.

To the questions she was constantly putting to herself, neither her own heart nor the silent woods where she wandered, struggling with her problems, could give answer. She longed to explain her secret to someone who might understand and advise her. Hence it was that she proved not unreceptive when Michel urged her to pay a call of her own on Father Athanase. The monk, he said, was very anxious to become better acquainted with her.

"He's not hoping to convert me?" she asked a little defiantly.

"By no means. Or at least not unless you ask him to. He respects everyone's right to believe as he sees fit. He is interested in you because you mean so much to me."

"O, he wants to find out whether I am worthy of you?"

"Don't distrust him, Adé; let him see how great a treasure you are to me."

Dom Athanase received her one morning in the visitors' room at the abbey. Michel had not accompanied her, guessing perhaps the secret desire she had to be alone with the monk. Thus she was able to lay bare frankly the fears which her husband's health and state of mind were causing her. As a matter of fact, it seemed to her that since they had come to Evolayne, Michel had been daily regaining his old strength and zest for life. The transformation which was taking place in him gave her pause for thought. Her mind turned seriously to the once vague project of establishing themselves in the country where Michel, the man of action but also the intellectual, might go on practicing medicine, and still have leisure for other studies. She was afraid that he might be hiding his desire for such a life of retirement because he felt that it would involve a sacrifice for her. With a priest, with his old friend, however, he would doubtless be more frank. Consequently she set about convincing the monk that for her part she had no attachment to the fashionable world, nor to Paris, and that wherever her husband would be happy, she would be. Dom Athanase listened to her attentively but without giving her the advice she sought. He confessed that Michel did not seem to him to be completely happy. But any hasty solution presented great risks. He promised to study his friend and tell Adélaide the result of his observations.

Their common solicitude for a person whom they both cherished drew them together. They saw each other several times after that, and discussed more general subjects. The priest's conversation was spirited and witty. The gayety of his character greatly astonished Adélaide. Religious natures interested her; she thought of them as extremely complex. As soon as she dared, she questioned the monk about his vocation. She supposed that he must have gone

34

through a period of doubt and struggle about which it would be interesting to hear. But either because he did not wish to speak of those difficulties, or because he had forgotten or surmounted them, Dom Athanase made no allusion to them. Instead he told a quite simple story. When he was very young he had heard the call of the Church. He had entered the abbey when he was twenty, never to leave it again. Certainly the joy reflected in his glance, in his frank laughter, in his sometimes boyish high spirits, was no mask. Burdened as he was with heavy responsibilities, he carried them effortlessly, rejoicing in life with the confident security of a child over whom his father is watching. Adélaide compared this unwavering, imperturbable serenity with her own so troubled happiness.

"I envy you a little, Father," she confessed one day, in a tone of melancholy.

It seemed as if the monk had long been waiting for those words, and had his reply prepared, so promptly did he answer:

"One doesn't envy a man warming himself in the sun, when one has only to step out of the shadows and enjoy what is freely offered to all."

Adélaide felt the attack coming, but she did not try to escape it. She thought that they knew each other well enough now to explain their religious positions in a friendly way. So when he asked her:

"You were once a Catholic, were you not?" she replied without embarrassment.

"By birth and education, yes. I have been baptized and I was brought up in a convent. I was married in the Church."

"But you no longer practice your religion?"

"No."

"Why not?"

She made a vague gesture. It was impossible for her to summon any feeling of tenderness or regret in thinking of the faith of her childhood. Its teachings had not lifted up her soul, they had stifled it, and her heart had always been indifferent or antagonistic to them. Religion to her had meant nothing but a collection of harsh dogmas, of narrow principles which her step-mother had used as a means of enforcing her authority over her and of smothering her spirits. Her youth had rebelled against the routine of the offices and the sacraments. She had abandoned them all abruptly when she left her step-mother's, and it had caused her neither struggle nor misgivings, for love had come just at that moment to give direction to her life. The fact that Michel did not attend Mass confirmed her in her tranquil incredulity. When later in her reading with him, she had come upon the integral Catholicism of men like Claudel, it had revived in her some respect for a doctrine which she had thought was dead.

"I admire religion as a source of poetry," she said,

"and I admit that I have failed to appreciate its nobility sometimes by feeling only its limitations."

"What philosophical system do you prefer?"

"None," she said with some embarrassment. "No doubt all of them contain some portion of truth, but not the whole truth; that lies too deeply hidden for our minds."

"Then you are content to remain in uncertainty, you don't seek the key to the mystery?"

The priest's questions were clipped, precise. Once he had proposed them, his lips closed tightly. He leaned forward a little toward Adélaide, as if to listen to the secret pounding of her heart. When she hesitated in her reply, he went on insistently:

"Nevertheless we have a problem to resolve here on earth. Do you never think of death?"

He looked at her attentively for a moment. Because his eyes were usually lowered, this glance came as a surprise to her, like an act of inexcusable impoliteness. It was a glance which pierced through superficialities to her inmost being. The monk noted the little tremor which passed over her. He saw an old, half-forgotten anguish come flooding back to her mind.

"Death!" she said, and her voice trembled. "For four years I thought of nothing else. For four years during the war when Michel was at the front, when he might have been killed at any moment."

"What would you have done then?"

"I had made up my mind. If he had died, I would have joined him."

She knew that remark was sinful. However it seemed to her that the priest would be disarmed by such a love, knowing how worthy of it Michel was, and that he would have only indulgence and forgiveness and secret esteem for her in spite of it. Accustomed as he was to hearing confessions, Father Athanase betrayed no sign of surprise, but his reply was a condemnation.

"Join him! Where? Do you imagine that the same paradise awaits those who die from courage and those who die from cowardice, for the hero and the criminal, for him who gives up his life in noble sacrifice, and him who takes his life by his own hand?"

She reddened, disconcerted. Up until this moment she had felt assured of the monk's sympathy and she was astonished that he did not understand her.

"You are a harsh judge," she said with dignity. "There are countries where they admire a wife who does not choose to survive her husband. What is cowardice in your eyes can be called fidelity and heroism."

Dom Athanase shook his head as if confronted by a sin which became more grievous at every word.

"Then Michel is the only thing that counts in your life? You recognize no other duty save that toward him? He is the absolute master of your soul, its only guiding principle? Is this life in which he has been given you sufficient for you?"

She made a gesture of dissent. She was less concerned now in answering the monk than she was in questioning her own heart, in trying to understand the mystery of her love which was always demanding more than was given her.

"No," she protested dully, "no, this life is not sufficient for me. It is too short and too imperfect for my love for him. I need eternity for that."

"Ah," cried the monk, prompt to seize on the slightest faltering in his adversary. "You admit eternity then?"

"You see," she said, her eyes full of tears, for she was thinking back to the cruelest hours of her life, "when I knew that Michel was close to the front and I heard from him so rarely, I sometimes thought that he was dead, and yet not that he was dead entirely. I felt that a bullet or a shell could only destroy a part of him, and that my love for him could never die either. O, I believe we are creatures of a just God, but He is far off, inaccessible. It is all so very obscure."

"You do not seek the light!"

"Perhaps not," she confessed, for the discussion was torturing her. "But man is not capable of understanding the infinite. So why struggle with problems that we cannot solve? We should live in the pres-

ent—" though she did not succeed in doing so—
"Michel and I are alive and happy!"

The priest sighed.

"What danger there is in happiness! It is like a
greenhouse in which the soul loses its fiber even while
it seems to flourish. Open the window, let a little
fresh air blow over it, and it withers, then dies completely."

Once more, Adélaide thought she heard a secret
warning in her heart and all about her, a dull rumbling in the clouds and under the earth presaging
the collapse of the refuge in which she lived. She
rose hastily to her feet.

"Father, if you don't mind, we shall not talk about
it any more."

He looked at her a last time with profound sadness.

"How afraid you are of truth," he said.

All day she had a feeling of unrest and unhappiness the exact cause of which escaped her but which
she attributed to her vexation at having found a
judge in the man she had believed to be her friend.
Father Athanase's severity had wounded her and she
complained of it to Michel. But instead of sharing
her feeling, the latter defended the monk.

"You must admit, Adé, that his attitude was perfectly logical. How could you expect to find in a
priest, who is convinced of a truth for which he has
sacrificed everything, the same impartial amiability

40

that goes with indifference? If he had the indulgent sympathy for your incredulity that you have for his faith, his life would lose its meaning and there would be nothing for him but to give up his orders. For him the world in which we are living is a battlefield where he must fight unceasingly for God's cause and where even in his charity he must tolerate error."

In a few words, very simply, he explained the point of view which so astonished Adélaide, and showed her wherein she was wrong. Wiser, less exacting than she in his relations with others, Michel always sought to understand rather than to be understood himself. He possessed to a high degree the faculty of putting himself in the place of people who did not resemble him, and of judging them objectively. That was the reason, doubtless, why he had been able to keep Father Athanase's friendship, and why in spite of their divergent opinions, the intimacy of the two men increased daily.

III. THE abbey of Evolayne was not only a place of pilgimage, it was a spiritual refuge to which men came from far away, priests and laymen, young men and old, to seclude themselves for a few days at a time while they sought contact once more with the eternal. The cloister separated them from the world, even from their memories. Daily cares lost their hold upon them, their hearts were lightened and were bathed in God's loving kindness. Dom Athanase affirmed that every soul, whether indifferent or ardent, happy or troubled, could find benefit in this retreat in the bosom of silence.

One morning as he was waiting for a group who were to enter upon such a retreat, he invited Michel to join them and spend a whole week within the abbey. He made the suggestion quite informally in the presence of Adélaide, and her husband, visibly tempted, looked at her questioningly. She manifested no surprise or unwillingness. She herself would have liked to have had an opportunity to share the monks' life and to observe them intimately, and she urged him heartily to accept the priest's offer.

During Michel's absence, she abandoned her daily

trips to the monastery and instead fell into the habit of walking over to the other side of the ridge where half a mile further away the convent of Helmancourt sheltered the daughters of Saint Benedict. The two cloisters were very different. The first accessible to everyone, vast and imposing, dominated the countryside; the other, hidden away, unknown to tourists, surrounded by massive walls and screened by a curve of the hill, was a symbol of the self-effacement of the women who dwelt within its walls. The nuns, invisible behind the grilles, participated in the offices by a distant chant, sustained and pure. Their voices, less impersonal and disciplined than those of the monks, betrayed by their inflections their individual souls. Adélaide sometimes thought she caught in them an avowal of ecstasy or distress, of supplication or reproach. She tried to imagine the existence of those recluses, pouring out their souls at the feet of a God who never replied to them. At least their God was always watching over them, gathering to Himself all their inmost thoughts, while she, tramping in the woods, could not hope to convey to Michel the love and longing that overflowed her heart. He would never know, even if she tried to tell him, how perfectly, here in the calm of the countryside and the evening, she had loved him.

The sixth day, she climbed the path to meet him. The hunger for his presence made her weak as if she had been starving. As soon as she caught a glimpse of him approaching, she stopped to wait. He was walking rapidly and did not seem to notice her until he was almost upon her. Then he gave a sudden start of surprise, as if for the whole week he had scarcely thought of her. As he kissed her, she had a vivid impression that he drew back defensively. It was as if he had been away a long time, so changed and different he seemed from the man who had taken leave of her a week before. What was the reason for that look of peace and of suffering in his eyes? What offense had he to reproach her for, that he should look at her with that expression of pitying indulgence and forgiveness as she replied to his question? She asked him in turn:

"How did you like it?"

"Very much," he said briefly, and in his voice seemed to be a determination to give no details concerning his retreat.

"Wasn't it very rigorous physically, the monastic life?" she insisted.

"The body adapts itself quickly. There is an atmosphere of joy and fulfillment that gives strength."

"I understand," she said. "How beautiful their chimera is!"

He seemed to find her remark out of place, and replied with a note of severity:

"It is really too easy to call everything a chimera which you do not understand."

Doubtless, Adélaide thought, living with the

monks, seeing their happiness close at hand had inspired Michel with the same feeling of admiration and envy which she had felt in her visit with Father Athanase. But he was not one like herself to give in to emotions without trying to analyze them and justify them. He tried to sift out the element of truth that lay back of every honest error. The thought came to her mind that later, when they were very old, if they had found nothing more satisfying, they might perhaps both die in the Catholic faith out of horror for absolute negation.

Consequently she was not astonished that Michel should give serious study to a religion which made so many men happy, or that he should spend days poring over books of theology and church history in the library of the abbey. She herself, attracted more by what appeals to the heart and the imagination and the senses than by what is directed to the intelligence alone, was predominantly interested in the rites and ceremonies and liturgy, and she followed the offices with considerable regularity. Michel no longer attended the conventual Mass, but early each morning, while she was still sleeping, went up to the abbey for low Mass which he found more beautiful and more moving than the high. One day, wakened sooner than usual, she heard him leaving. The desire to surprise him vanquished her laziness. She rose, dressed quickly and followed shortly after him.

With happy step she climbed the path, for the

45

cool, bracing air stimulated her and her spirits were lifted up with the joy of the morning. Shafts of golden sunlight shot across the pale, glistening sky. The dancing breeze shook the leaves and the grass and from the bushes came the drone of a thousand turbulent little lives. The humming and chirping mingled in a single song of glory, as if each creature were giving joyous thanks for the gift of life.

At first glance, when she entered, the abbey seemed empty. The great altar in the choir, reserved for the solemn ceremonies, was deserted at this hour. But in each of the side chapels, lifeless in the middle of the day, a monk, served by some novice or lay brother, was officiating. At the left, at the end of the lateral nave, a chapel larger than the others and raised some steps above the floor, was set apart for the faithful who wished to partake in the Holy Sacrifice. A dozen women and a few men were occupying the sparse benches and Adélaide recognized from the distance Michel's tall figure. She did not wish to join him, but knelt at the foot of the steps so that the transept separated them. Turning a little from side to side, she could see other altars. The Masses were not all being celebrated at the same time. Here a monk, drawing up the white amice over his head, was leaving one of the chapels where, a few moments later, another figure exactly like him took his place. There a priest, his arms extended, was saying the preface, while another, bent over the altar stone, was partaking of the Body of his Lord. They did not hasten through the sacred rite as do parish priests; each prayer came slowly from the depths of their hearts to their scarcely moving lips. Their faces, so impassive, were like the faces of men entranced. Their eyes opened only to read the prayers in the missal, then closed again quickly, shutting out all other images. Beside them stood the servers—novices not yet empowered to consecrate, lay brothers who never would perform the miracle of transubstantiation—profoundly respectful as they assisted the celebrant, the father, endowed with a power that was infinite. And from the fourteen chapels distributed throughout the immense edifice, the little bells sounded, answered each other, as to right and to left the Host was elevated, now at this altar, now at that. The sacrifice offered for the redemption of the world never ceased. The atmosphere was charged with a sense of the miraculous. Adélaide had no sensation of antagonism. She understood that Michel came here each morning in search of strong, pure impressions which he would carry with him throughout the day. She congratulated herself on having made the necessary effort, this once at least, to share his emotions. Later, when they had left Evolayne, they would often re-live this hour together.

As she was looking at him, from the distance, joining her thoughts with his, she saw him rise. The Mass was not yet ended. The priest who was celebrating it was standing motionless, bent over the chalice. The little bell had just sounded three times. She was astonished that Michel was leaving so soon. But instead of coming down toward her, as she expected, slowly he mounted toward the altar. She had straightened up, feeling that she must be dreaming. The priest, carrying the ciborium, was now facing him and advancing to the communion rail. Michel, kneeling with the faithful, received the host and came back to his place, his arms crossed, his head bowed, his eyes cast down.

It was then, in a blinding revelation, that he appeared to her, wholly changed, wholly different from her, a convert, a believer, tenderly carrying his God in the heart that she thought she knew so well, but which had been willing to hold such a secret from her. A feeling of incredible outrage swept through her, and her love writhed and cried out in torment. In the instant everything in the abbey became hostile to her: the golden crucifix shining in the light, the figures of the saints in the stained glass, the Host which was being elevated in a chapel on her right, the priests bowed in prayer by their altars, occupied in invoking she knew not what kind of sorcery that was robbing her of all she loved.

She hurried from the church and found herself outside in the dazzling light of the court. The sun, her enemy now, was riddling her with burning arrows. Her thoughts whirled, smote against each other, mad, uncontrollable. She wanted both to flee from her husband and to crush him with her reproaches. In her fever and confusion she made a thousand different resolutions.

The wisest would have been to go back to the inn and hide her discovery. She should have left Michel the merit of making a free avowal, or, if he persisted in his silence, the shame of his hypocrisy. But Adélaide knew how to practice neither patience nor pretense. She felt herself incapable of seeming to be ignorant when anger was shaking her very being and so many bitter words were rushing to her lips. Emotion, to which she always listened, spoke louder than reason. She waited for Michel.

Apparently he was prolonging his devotions, for a number of communicants had already left the abbey. At length he came out, one of the last, and stood for a moment by the portal, blinking his eyes in the bright light. He was smiling, not at a living person, but at the vision that was within him, at the pale, empty sky where he discerned the presence which he worshiped. Adélaide was torn with jealousy at that smile which was not for her. He did not see her, or rather she was still nothing but an anonymous figure to him. He came down the steps without self-consciousness. Then when he had come almost up to her, he recognized her. Habituated as a doctor to bending over the sick, to discovering the death, visible to himself alone, hidden in apparently healthy

49

frames, he knew how to hide his reactions. His face showed no surprise at meeting his wife there at that unaccustomed hour, only a determination to discuss nothing. Immediately, negligently, he put the one important question:

"Are you just coming?"

Before she spoke, her face betrayed her. Scorn, humiliation, indignation, sarcasm trembled one after the other over her features.

"No," she said, "I am leaving. I attended Mass, as you did."

He understood, reddened a little, held a hesitant hand toward her, then as she turned from him, suggested:

"Shall we go back?"

They crossed the level expanse in front of the abbey and started down the path. Michel, ill at ease before her silence, attempted the first words that came into his head.

"It's going to be a beautiful day, hot probably, but this early in the morning the breeze . . ."

She made a gesture to him to be silent. She could not tolerate his thus escaping all explanation. Did he not hear the dull rumbling and crashing within her as her whole life crumbled and fell in ruins? She stumbled on. The path before her fell away like a waterfall, the grass reached up to the sky, the light broke in a thousand facets in her eyes. Her face was livid, she was blinded with tears and the pounding of her blood.

"I congratulate you on your conversion," she burst out.

Those few words comforted her a little. Her tears overflowed. Michel misjudged the cause of her grief.

"Really, Adé, does it make you as angry as that?"

She was walking close to him without looking at him. She spoke with a fierce bitterness, forcing herself not to cry.

"Whether you turned Christian, or Mohammedan or Buddhist, I wouldn't stand in your way. But that such a transformation could have taken place in you, that you could have had such a complete change of heart, without your deigning to tell me anything about it, that I can scarcely believe. I have never deserved an affront like that. Are you so ashamed of your conversion that you have to hide it from me? Or, more likely, are you ashamed of me in front of your God? Am I so frivolous, so degraded, that you don't think I am worthy to be associated in your spiritual life? At least, I have found out your new faith and your scorn of me both at once. Nothing in you belonged to me but a shell. Your soul disregarded me completely, it sought its happiness outside of me, excluded me from its paradise. I would rather have forgiven you physical infidelity!"

She stopped to catch her breath. Michel saw another tear run down her cheek.

"When you are more calm and can listen to me," he began . . .

"I am perfectly calm," she interrupted furiously, "and even if I weren't, it's all very easy to blame someone for not being calm when you have just insulted her. . . . But go on, say something. . . . I can listen to you. . . ."

"I am not blaming you for anything, Adé," he said, his voice composed and very gentle. "I understand the pain I have given you. I should have liked to have shared the great, ineffable secret of my conversion, and I can imagine your shock when you discovered it just now. But the way in which grace manifests itself is a mysterious, incommunicable thing, which would have been incomprehensible to you. You would have asked explanations. What could I have said to you? From the first evening of our stay here, I have been transformed. You thought I was praying out of courtesy to the monks, out of respect for their faith. No. I prayed because I felt God, who is still hidden from you, living within me, an undeniable, dazzling presence. One does not explain a miracle. One says: come and see. But if the miracle is within, even that is impossible. Your human eyes could not have perceived what I was carrying in my heart. So I kept silent, trying to guard this treasure, to do all that I could to make sure that it would not be taken from me. I have had to examine myself unsparingly, to seek in turn Him who sought me, to strengthen my belief and make my decision. Such a new conception of life cannot be achieved in the midst of words and discussions. O, if only you could have found Him as I did, if only the conversion of both of us could have taken place at the same time! I have never ceased to implore God for that grace. But, alas, I have had no sign to give me hope that it might be granted to me. Before secluding myself in the abbey to become a Christian once more, I begged Father Athanase to examine you. He told me: 'She is not hostile, she is indifferent, she is satisfied with her present happiness, she has no concern for the eternal salvation. There is only one fissure in the perfect edifice of her security where grace may eventually enter.' So I did not dare reveal my conversion to you. I was afraid of your indignation, of your mockery."

She listened to him, piling up new grievances.

"So," she flung at him, "you had to have an intermediary between us. You had to have that priest, whom I had never seen two months ago, explain my soul to you. After seven years of marriage, during which I haven't had a thought or an emotion that was hidden from you, I am still so profound a stranger to you that to read into my heart you have to depend on someone else. You think that a woman who loves you, who lives in you, must always be a closed book to you? You should have known me well enough to realize that I always make myself love what you love, and that any religion which you might adopt would never be an object of scorn or mockery with me. That should have been enough to begin with. There was no need to raise such a barrier of mystery between us, but that monk persuaded you otherwise."

"You are mistaken. On the contrary, the Father has urged me daily to tell you everything. I could not make up my mind to it. How was I to explain to you? . . . I don't talk easily. I cannot open up my heart. . . ."

"Except when you are in love," she said, remembering how he had confided in her, sometimes, when he had been in her arms.

"That is just it, I am in love! . . ." he murmured very softly. "You see from the moment one believes in Him, God is no vague concept, He is a being that one loves and one cannot accept His being nothing to others."

"I would have understood," she sighed.

"Alas, you see very well that you would not have, and knowing your attitude . . ."

"Why, let me ask you again, did you choose that priest to reveal it to you?"

"Understand me, Adé. Once one accepts religion, one accepts it unreservedly, one admits the authority of the priest and his competence, because of the special powers indissolubly attached to his ministry. Your heart, yes, I think I know it. But to search the innermost parts of your soul, to understand your exact position in regard to religious matters, the Father is better qualified than I; that is why I wanted him to question you."

"O," she cried, shuddering. "Why all these subtleties? My soul was no fortress barred against you, with mysterious hideaways and secret locks. It was a house where you could open every door at your wish. You had no need of anyone to help you force a single one. But what is the use of explaining to you what perfect trust is?"

They had arrived in front of the station. Instead of keeping on toward the inn, Adélaide turned to the right on the highway which led up between the wooded slopes of the valley. Michel wished to accompany her, but she stopped him:

"Please leave me," she said. "I want to be by myself."

A few minutes later she turned into a narrow path which led up into the forest, and climbed it rapidly. Soon there was nothing about her but trees and grass and silence and nature. For a long time she half-walked and half-ran, trying to tire the anger within her, until at length she dropped on the ground and buried her grief-stricken face in the deep, unanswering soil as if it were a friendly shoulder. Then the cry burst from her which summed up all her sorrow, all her pain:

"He doesn't love me!"

IV.

WILLFULLY, knowing that Michel detested unpunctuality, she made herself late for luncheon. He was waiting for her, seated under an arbor in front of the inn, and he offered no criticism for he saw that she was not coming back to him pacified. Her face was calm, but her eyes, like those of a caged beast, still shone with fury at the unpardonable offense she had suffered.

Michel's efforts to engage her in conversation were in vain. By the curtness of her replies she refused even the semblance of reconciliation.

"Did you have a good walk?"

"Very good."

"Where did you go?"

"Over there."

"Did you sit down and rest?"

"A little."

He was visibly losing patience. His nostrils flared. A vein at his temple turned purple and began to pulsate. She knew those danger signals.

"You're a pleasant companion!" he murmured between his teeth.

"Yes," she said, goading him. "Happily, however,

56

your honor will force you to put up with me all the rest of your life."

She trembled a little at thus defying him. Never had he permitted her to take that acrimonious, insulting tone with him. In all their disputes he met her fits of temper with a violence colder, more disciplined, and therefore more effective, than her own. To her great surprise he dropped his head and said without bitterness:

"I cannot quarrel with you."

Instantly, she felt it was not she to whom he was yielding. It was to that God whom he loved better than he had ever loved her. Unwilling as he had always been to hurt her, he had never been able to master his imperious temper in order to spare her.

During the following days that impression became conviction. Normally, when Michel had not been able to control himself during some altercation, he waited in proud silence for her to beg his pardon. But now the rôles were reversed. It was she who remained caustic and aloof, he who multiplied his attentions, his thoughtfulness, who seemed tacitly to admit his wrongdoing and the justice of her grievance. In accordance with her interpretation, Adélaide found it no proof of tenderness, but of obedience to the laws of the Church and the commands of Father Athanase. Moreover, for Michel to be so tolerant must mean that their rupture was a matter of indifference to him. Seeing him always so unruffled, she thought he was happy and she was miserable that he should be so except in her. Much as she loved him, and in spite of her conviction that she would never succeed, she set out to destroy that happiness. Instead of sparing him, as she had always done before, she tried consciously to wound him. One day he pressed her to go with him to the abbey to attend one of the offices.

"Why should I go with you?" she replied cuttingly. "I don't go with you when you go to see your patients. You are a doctor and I am not. Why should I go to church? You are a believer and I am not."

She felt an aversion amounting to horror for the abbey, detested it as a rival. Michel guessed her jealousy and reproached himself for having abandoned her so frequently. On several occasions he tried to accompany her on the long walks that she seemed to like, but she sent him back.

"Leave nature to me and keep your God. It is evident that you find Him quite sufficient for you."

All their relations were strained and artificial now. They no longer found anything to say to each other. They read different books. They avoided speaking of Father Athanase or any religious question. Their only subject of conversation came from the letters they received and which they kept the habit of showing to each other. But the most innocent remark was enough to bring their discord to the surface. One day, during luncheon, Adélaide received a letter from

58

Maurice Verdon, her brother, who was spending his vacation in Deauville in gay company.

"As for you," he wrote to his sister, "I cannot imagine what you can be doing in that forsaken country with an abbey for your only distraction. You talk about the beauty of the offices. What fascination can you find in them? It's always the same thing: psalms and Latin and posturings. Such mummery in our own time seems scarcely conceivable."

"Good old Maurice, not much of a mystic in him," said Michel, folding up the letter.

He had put no malice in the remark. But Adélaide took offense and although she knew that she was very different from her brother, she immediately identified herself with him and pretended to believe that her husband's observation was a slight upon herself.

"We at least have good, solid common sense, both of us, even if we can't share your soul flights," she said acidly.

And, without thinking, but with the sole aim of displeasing Michel, she added:

"I want to go and finish my vacation in Deauville."

He looked at her uncertainly and asked:

"Is it true that the psalms and the Latin and the mummery, as Maurice calls it, bore you? I admit that the atmosphere of Evolayne is a little ascetic for a woman . . ."

"Particularly for someone as giddy and frivolous as I," she finished bitterly.

He went on without seeming to notice the interruption:

"It is perfectly natural that you should want some relaxation, and some gayety. If you like, we can do that, join Maurice after a little while."

"We?" she said, feigning intense surprise. "You would come with me?"

"What a question! My place is with you."

"Do you feel that you have to watch over me all the time? Don't you think Maurice is a sufficient protector?"

"O, certainly," he said, disconcerted. "If you prefer to go alone . . ."

"It would be a joyful deliverance for you," she finished with a provoking laugh.

This time, he lost patience. He was no saint. Under the goad of so many bitter, infuriating speeches, his anger boiled over.

"That's enough," he snapped savagely. "I can't say a word to you any more without your twisting the sense of it. I shall not tolerate it any longer."

"Really," she flung back ironically. "And what am I to do?"

"Keep quiet," he continued with crushing authority. But she did not flinch.

"It is most unfortunate," she said, "that they don't

require a vow of silence in marriage the way they do in some religious orders."

"At least there is the vow of obedience," he replied harshly, but there was now more of sadness than irritation in his manner. "I wouldn't have believed, Adélaide, that you could so wantonly destroy our happiness. You have made me suffer cruelly."

She did not reply, but turned her head away so that he would not see the defeat begin to show in her eyes.

As soon as luncheon was finished, she set out on her customary walk. But she did not go far. The heat was blazing. A strange languor pervaded her being and, coming to a clump of black pine, she dropped down on the brown carpet of needles. For a time she drowsed, then, her torpor leaving her, she found love suddenly reawakened within her. It had been ten days now since she had first quarreled with Michel, ten days since they had exchanged a tender word or a kiss, ten days that she had been struggling against him, perhaps with the idea in the back of her mind that she would find a greater pleasure in yielding. Suddenly she passed from pride to weakness, to utter submission. In their last encounter Michel had again won the upper hand. His cry, "You have made me suffer cruelly," proving to her that she could still wound that heart which she had believed insensible, plunged her into the depths of remorse. She thought back over her behavior and found she had been hateful and cowardly. He had not shown confidence in her, certainly. But she had punished him viciously, had put his new virtue to a bitter test. She had taken advantage of his resolution to be patient, in order to torment him unceasingly. She resolved to be different henceforth. This evening she would ask his forgiveness. She would make up for her faults.

At first thought, it all seemed very easy. Her anger flown, the hostility she had been nurturing for the last few days against Catholicism dropped from her. She determined to go back to the abbey, to follow the offices. Not only would she not hinder her husband in his devotions, but she would conform her own habits as much as possible to his, and force herself to try to understand his feelings. Then he would confide in her again. They would be happy in one another, in perfect harmony.

Here she fell afoul of a new obstacle, the real cause of the trouble. The intimacy whose return she so ardently desired could be reborn only on the condition that she and Michel agreed upon the main point at issue. Their hearts could never be attuned as long as she saw only falsity in what for Michel was supreme truth. And suddenly that barrier between them ceased to seem insurmountable to her. Was she really an atheist? No. She hated the narrow principles and intolerant piety of her step-mother, but the religion of a Claudel inspired her with a profound ad-

62

miration which might well change into belief. A passage from *La Messe là-bas* came to her mind:

*De quoi est-ce que le catéchisme nous parle et de
  quoi sont faites nos prières?*

*Un père de qui sont complètement ses fils, des enfants
  qui sont complètement à leur père.*

Des frères sous le même toit ensemble, une mère admirable et charmante . . .

She smiled, captivated. She felt like a child who has been abandoned and whose heart is warmed by the words which the poet offered: home and a mother *admirable et charmante*. . . . With deep concentration she began to go over the Credo:

I believe in God the Father Almighty, Creator of Heaven and Earth.

That first article she could accept without reservation. She had always believed that there existed a Supreme Being who was good and who ruled the universe.

And in Jesus Christ, His only Son, Our Lord.

She loved Him, who was crucified, more than anyone else who had suffered for the world, more than all the heroes and the sages. For her, as for everyone who accepts Him as God, He was the Being above all others worthy of adoration. And she remembered how, in reading Renan's book, it had pained her to find this great figure treated as purely human.

I believe in the Holy Ghost, the Holy Catholic Church . . .

63

Here, she fell into indifference. The Holy Ghost was a pretty concept about which she felt no conviction. The Church, which for the moment was personified for her in Father Athanase, seemed to her meddlesome and indiscreet, despite the fact that its tradition and its offices and its rites were not lacking in grandeur. She withheld judgment on these two articles and wound up:

The communion of Saints and the resurrection of the body.

To that she could adhere unreservedly, for the words promised reunion everlasting to those who loved each other on earth. They affirmed that she would never be separated from Michel.

All in all, she was almost a Christian, except for her repugnance at fulfilling the outward duties of a religion whose essential dogmas she accepted. But might it not be that this repugnance was the result of lack of familiarity or her own indolence rather than anything else? Though it seemed sufficient to her to worship the Father in spirit and in truth, she admitted that such theoretical worship possessed neither force nor warmth. If she had lived at the time of Christ, she would have thrown herself at His feet and would have implored Him for the grace of a more burning faith. The Church, through its sacraments, offered, to all the faithful, easy access to the Master. The doubts which still raised themselves within her might be vanquished by a single act of

humility and trust. She realized that a conversion demanded a preparation less summary than that which
she had just made so rapidly. She thought for a moment of consulting her husband and Father Athanase
but her hesitations were short-lived; her exaltation
carried everything before it. An overwhelming desire
for a reconciliation possessed her. She knew that she
could be truly at peace with Michel only if she returned to him with a soul regenerated, utterly submissive to the God whom he served.

The sun was just beginning to set when she
emerged from the woods and breathlessly she climbed
up the path to the abbey. The office was over for the
day and the nave deserted. Courageously she went
to the door of the sacristy and rang the bell, asking
for a confessor without designating anyone in particular. The monk who came was very old and
seemed not too inspiring. He asked her only vague
questions concerning the reasons for her return to
God. She admitted that above all she was desirous of
following her husband in his return to the practice of
his religion, and that her faith was not yet unwavering.

"Time will strengthen it," he affirmed. "You have
realized that the worldly life and worldly pleasures
cannot satisfy. You will soon understand the delights
which are offered by the life of the spirit. One who
had never seen other than electric light would think
such light beautiful. But show him the splendor of

the sun and he will not hesitate to declare it incomparably more beautiful, and he will wonder that he had ever been able to be content with the other. God, my child is the sun. Tomorrow, in communion, you will feel His presence, His warmth, His comfort, and you will no longer be able to tolerate the light from electric bulbs and candles."

He continued for some time in this vein. The banality of his words chilled Adélaide's fine enthusiasm, gave her a feeling of discouragement against which she rebelled as soon as she had left the confessional.

"A poet," she thought, "can talk uninspiredly about poetry without its ceasing to be great because of that. In the same way a priest can talk uninspiredly about God without His being the less lovable. Mediocrity is the rule in everything. One must accept it in religion as one does in art and follow one's own intelligence."

Besides, she would not be long without help. Soon she would have her husband for support and for spiritual guide. The very thought of it kindled a flame in her heart, and prayers began to burn there like a multitude of candles. She lost all idea of time, and opening her soul to God, she was astonished that she could have lived so long without Him within her. The only thing lacking in her joy was that she could not share it with Michel. But she had decided not to tell him of her conversion that evening. From

66

malice and from tenderness she wanted to prolong
their apparent misunderstanding so that he might
still suffer, so that he might be the happier. Fearing
she might betray herself, as soon as she returned to
the inn she shut herself up in her room with the
excuse that she had a headache.

Her vengeance was as perfect as it was magnanimous. She hid her heart as he had hidden his heart.
She took care the next day not to go up to the abbey
until after he had left. She found a place in the chapel
several rows behind him and it was only when they
both arose from the communion-rail, with a number
of people separating them, that he suddenly saw her
near him, her hands clasped. He came upon her as
she had come upon him, in the same solemn act, no
better prepared than she for the discovery. But where
she had felt only revolt, indignation, bitterness, he
was suffused with an unspeakable happiness for
which he thanked her with a single look. Strong as
was the shock he had received, he succeeded in controlling himself. His eyes lowered, he returned to
his bench, while she followed and knelt next to him.
Both immersed themselves in fervent prayer. The
little bells echoing softly through the nave of the
church, alone reminded them where they were.
Michel took Adélaide's hand and laid it against his
cheek, then covered it with both his own. She felt
that he was crying. Then she was overcome by an
emotion so infinitely soft and beautiful that she mis-

took it for God's grace. The love, which overwhelmed her, pure beyond reproach but human still, seemed to her a manifest sign of the divine presence. She marveled that one, poor act of humility should be rewarded with such fullness of faith, with such rapture. She felt akin to the saints, to the angels, cradled and borne aloft in peace as if in a strong, limpid sea. But her gratitude went primarily to the man who had shown her the way. She praised him in praising God. Then her own prayer of thanks broke off. It seemed to her that Michel's prayers were passing through her, were sufficient for them both. She added her fervor to them without knowing what they were.

They were the last to leave the abbey. Outside in the court where two weeks before they had exchanged such bitter words, they stopped. It was a gray, still day. A recent rain had set free the most delicate scents. The leaves and the grass and the soil and the bark of the trees perfumed the air like flowers. The world about them seemed wholly new: perfectly ordered, perfectly explained, blessed, divine. Their eyes looked wonderingly here and there, then sought each other. Adélaide had anticipated that their reconciliation would be accompanied by great effusiveness. But here she was standing in front of Michel, never thinking of embracing him, silent and calm, her head lifted a little toward him, for he was taller than she. Under his thick, dark lashes, his blue eyes rested on her tenderly, like the caress of the sun through leaves. Like a flower, her soul lifted to the warmth, opened to let it penetrate her. In ineffable peace and understanding their thoughts became one.

"Michel," she stammered, "what has come over me? Never have I loved you so. . . ."

"Nor I," he murmured. "I love you so much more deeply than ever before! You see, no human love can have any reality except in God. I understand today for the first time the mystic sense of marriage, its eternal grandeur. Our union was imperfect. I feel as if it were only today, this morning, that I married you."

She drew a deep breath at the everlasting happiness which was opening up before her. At last and for the first time she experienced that feeling of security which had hitherto always been lacking in their love.

With her arm in her husband's, she went with him down the path. Every tree, every detail of her surroundings reminded her of the day of their quarrel.

"Can you forgive me, Michel?" she asked humbly. "I don't deserve it, I was so loathsome, so hateful. . . ."

"That is all passed, Adé. You have just given me a joy which I no longer dared hope for. I am still stunned. O, my darling, how did it happen?"

She no longer regarded her conversion as having taken place the afternoon before, in a few hours, in the forest. Running over in her mind all the emotions which she had felt since coming to Evolayne, she lent them a new significance, and, identifying herself with Michel, she believed she had always been in perfect harmony with him.

"I, too, have had my road to Damascus. The revelation came to me at the same time that it did to you. But a woman has a greater instinct of resistance. She takes fright and flees from what she desires. When she even resists the man she loves and who she knows loves her, how can she be expected to yield to God without a struggle?"

"At least," he cried joyfully, "you can't reproach me any more for having hidden my conversion from you. Because you have taken an infernal delight in concealing your own spiritual state from me."

"That's true," she said, laughing. "I was taking vengeance on you, an eye for an eye. Up until this morning I could do that. But now I am going to have to be a model wife. You will see how obedient and considerate and tender and loving I shall be!"

"It sounds promising."

"You don't seem convinced."

"No. I know how your mood can change."

"Your own has certainly been unruffled and serene enough. And to tell the truth, Michel, I'm not sure I like this new patience of yours; it has worn me out recently. I'll let you still get angry if you'll let me too. . . ."

"O, no, no! I want a tender, loving wife. I've had enough bitterness."

"Are we always going to live under a cloudless sky, in a monotony of perfect righteousness and perfect harmony? It sounds extraordinarily dull to me."

"That is a subversive opinion."

"O, is it? Then I withdraw it."

Their happiness changed to gayety, but one so profound, so rapturous that sometimes in the midst of their laughter they looked at each other with tears in their eyes.

V. THAT same day, after vespers, Michel joyfully announced the news of Adélaide's conversion to Father Athanase. The monk received the information with some surprise.

"It's remarkably quick," he said, shaking his head. "When I questioned her, there was nothing to indicate that she might soon become a Christian again."

"Yet she was one already," Michel offered eagerly. "Her hesitation in avowing it is easy to understand. I wouldn't have opened my soul so readily if you hadn't been an old friend. She didn't know you. She was touched by grace at the same time as I, but she was afraid and she had no one to guide her. She had to struggle with her difficulties alone. My lack of confidence in her prolonged her resistance."

"Be that as it may," said the priest, "she will need the counsel of a priest now. I am entirely at her disposition."

Michel could scarcely hope that Adélaide, irritated by what she regarded as the monk's interference, would accept him as her spiritual director. But much to his surprise she received the offer, which he transmitted to her, without hostility. In the meekness of her return to God, she recognized the injustice of her grievances against the monk and preferred to entrust herself to him rather than to the prosaic, unenlightened priest who had heard her confession. In the course of several interviews, she opened her soul to him with perfect frankness.

Father Athanase could find in her conversion little more than human motives. But he knew that God does not always use supernatural means to touch men's hearts. Adélaide's sincerity was patent. She wanted to let the spirit of Christianity enter into her, to act and think henceforth as a Catholic.

It all seemed very easy at first. From the point of view of ethics, she was already living a Christian life. Her passion for her husband was permissible. Her new beliefs demanded only the most trivial of sacrifices. She forced herself to rise early in the morning, to receive communion frequently; and it was no effort at all to resume the habit of prayer. But there were certain practices against which she still rebelled.

"The rosary bores me," she confessed. "It's always the same; at the end of ten *Aves* my mind wanders. . . ."

The priest showed himself indulgent:

"The rosary has its virtues, monotonous as it may seem. But never mind, pray as you like."

"He is really charming," she said to herself, vanquished.

73

And he, in his turn, recognized in her a soul endowed at least with good will.

But their mutual sympathy was of short duration. The monk was not long in discovering Adélaide's abysmal ignorance of religious doctrine. Her faith was still that of the heart alone and he required that it be of the mind as well. Thus, at their regular interviews at the abbey he began to talk to her more as a theologian than as a mystic, applying himself to abstract exposition of the great truths which she must henceforth accept. One morning, when he was discoursing to her on the unity of the Church, which, in his eyes, proved more conclusively than any other argument the excellence and divinity of the Catholic doctrine, she objected:

"Father, I want very much to believe in this unity. But what a difference there is between the broad, tolerant religion of yours and Michel's, and the teachings we used to receive in the convent. There, they poisoned our minds with outworn superstitions like hell and eternal damnation . . ."

The monk stopped her with a gesture accompanied by that piercing look which never failed to unsettle her.

"You say 'outworn superstitions'?"

"Yes, of course," she answered disconcerted.

The priest's face showed a severity not devoid of mockery.

"It is your impression, doubtless, that little by lit-

74

tle the Church has evolved so that now there is no longer any question of hell, only a heaven benevolently open to all?"

"I think," she replied with conviction, "that the Church still makes use of the idea of hell to frighten the miserable souls for whom love wouldn't be a sufficient motive for living upright lives. But I do not believe that anyone who thinks about it seriously, who is truly compassionate, can accept the idea of damnation. That there should be some punishment in the next world for evildoers seems necessary, but how can we reconcile our minds to an eternal punishment for sins in this transitory life?"

"Still you admit eternal reward for those who lead equally transitory lives of virtue?"

"It doesn't seem absolutely just," she admitted loyally, "but is it not fitting that God's judgments should show an excess of mercy, rather than of severity? Father, you do not mean to tell me that you believe in hell?"

"As firmly as I do in my own life," he said, smiling at her astonishment.

Her anger blazed.

"And you can be at peace," she cried, "knowing that so many poor souls, your fellow men, your friends, your own flesh and blood, may fall into that Gehenna? You can picture a serene, exclusive heaven where the elect will not be troubled by the screams of agony from below, by the endless torture of their brothers? Where is your heart? Where is your feeling for others? For myself I would rather be with the accursed. If I believed in hell, I would want to be damned."

"Regrettable," murmured the monk between his teeth. "Nevertheless you must believe in it."

"Everything in me recoils from it; I refuse."

"Very well, in that case you are not a Christian."

"I am certainly more of a Christian than you," she flung at him, deliberately addressing him as a man, not as a representative of God.

Accustomed to directing more docile souls, Father Athanase was amazed at such independence. Tolerant as he was toward little things, he became inflexible as soon as the dogmas of the Church came into question. The two faced each other, he very calm yet unyielding, she trembling with anger.

"What you do not seem to understand," he said, holding her with those eyes of his, "is that your conversion carries with it, if it is sincere, certain obligations which you cannot escape; among others, absolute submission to the authority of the Church and to revealed truth. You are not free to accept this and reject that according to your likes and dislikes. You must take everything or reject everything together. It is true that certain texts in the Scripture may be interpreted differently, but Christ's words concerning hell are numerous and explicit."

"For myself I regard them only as imagery."

"There you fall into the error of private interpretation and Protestantism. Moreover the Church has declared her position by including hell among its dogmas. I repeat, a Catholic has no liberty in this matter. If you do not believe in hell, you must accuse yourself of it in confession, you will be classed as a heretic and no priest will give you absolution."

"Very well," she said, rising to leave. "I shall have to reflect upon it."

She thought of the priest as being little short of mad, and she hurried to seek out her husband so that she might share her indignation with him.

"Why, he's five hundred years behind the times, your Father Athanase," she cried. "He's the most cruel, most narrow-minded man in the world."

Step by step, she went over their controversy, convinced that Michel would take her view. He listened without betraying the least surprise and when she told him the monk's parting words, he nodded.

"Nothing could be more obvious. We must either accept the doctrine in its entirety or reject it. The act of faith—'I believe all the truths which the Holy Catholic Church believes and teaches, because Thou, O Lord, hast revealed them'—admits no qualification."

For a moment she was mute with astonishment.

"But, Michel," she said finally, "you yourself are always excusing every sort of fault and wrongdoing, you are so indulgent of human weakness, your heart is so full of pity, how can you admit a Creator who would damn his creatures for eternity?"

"Understand me," he replied, "I have no sympathy with that specter-like concept of God which some fanatical souls make use of to terrify others—an angry, relentless God whose wrath they call down at any provocation, convinced of salvation for themselves. We have no right to believe that we are without stain, nor to judge others. But nonetheless, there are sins so vile, so heinous, that even pity does not shrink from meting out a terrible punishment for them. I have often seen you horrified at some act of cruelty, Adé. Think of the tyrants, the kings, the rulers of the earth, whose greatest delight it was to spill human blood. They inflicted unspeakable tortures. They laughed at the sight of their brothers being burned and crucified and torn on the rack. No martyrdom was long enough to satisfy them. Do they deserve the mercy which they refused to grant to others?"

The crime of cruelty had in truth always seemed almost unforgivable to her. But one of Victor Hugo's verses came to her lips:

Un monstre est un infirme et l'infirme a ses droits.

Michel nodded.

"God takes the weakness into account. Perhaps it's the result of lack of intelligence or imagination, or the intoxication of power. All that is weighed by divine justice. But while we are on the subject of

Hugo, doesn't he say somewhere that every sinner fixes his own punishment?"

She had a quick memory for poetry. The passage Michel was thinking of came to her:

L'assassin pâlirait s'il voyont sa victime:
C'est lui. L'oppresseur vil, le tyran sombre et fou,
En frappant sans pitié sur tous, forge le clou
Qui le clouera dans l'ombre au fond de la matière.

She began to understand. Every truth beautifully expressed found its way easily to her heart and won her fervent acceptance. Yet, as she ran over the *Bouche d'Ombre* in her mind, that poem which had been the wellspring of hers and Michel's religious thought, she saw those errant souls, long prisoners of their crimes, struggling upward until they found the road to paradise once more.

"But in the poem," she said, "doesn't Hugo make it all end at last in complete forgiveness and harmony?"

Et Jésus se penchant sur Bélial qui pleure,
Lui dira: C'est donc toi!

Michel cherished that poem; he could not condemn it:

"Bélial qui pleure," he repeated, weighting the last words, "is no longer simply Bélial. The tears are a sign of repentance. Every sin, every act of wrongdoing which is truly repented of is already at least partially forgiven. Your heart is too full of love, Adé, to understand that there are certain souls which are

79

dominated by hate, by the hate of God and of good and of everything which is fine. They obstinately seek that which is evil. They resist God's grace, they desire no forgiveness. God would open his heaven to them in vain. They would refuse to enter it. He does not have to intervene. They flee of their own accord from His intolerable love into the depths of hell. Every virtue lightens the soul, lifts it up. Every fault is a weight dragging it down into the abyss."

Adélaide sighed:

"It is a sad world, and once I thought it was so beautiful."

That was the first cloud on the horizon of peace and splendor which religion had opened to her. The dogma of hell suggested other doubts on the origin of pain and evil. She questioned Father Athanase. His answer was frank:

"Don't look to me for an absolutely satisfactory explanation. Theologians have all wrestled in vain with this problem of pain and evil. Into this world, created by a perfect God, a disorder has been introduced which cannot be His work and which must therefore be the work of His creature. And that is bound up with the question of free will."

"But," she cried, rebellious once more, "God should have known that man would sin. Why did He allow him such a dangerous freedom? What would you say of a mother who let her child play with a burning torch?"

"That she was acting imprudently, if he was very young. But she would be no less at fault if, after he was old enough to be able to discern for himself, she should forbid him all initiative. On the one hand there is the fire which burns and destroys, but which also gives light and heat; there is water which drowns, but which also washes and quenches thirst. There is the weapon which wounds and which protects, the wine which intoxicates but strengthens, there is love which may damn or save, and there are the sins which no one must commit. She must warn him against all dangers; then he must take the responsibility himself. God gave man a conscience and His commandments for guidance. But He showed great respect for His creature in allowing him the possibility of choice. If He had opened but one path to him, if He had not permitted him to disobey, He would have held him in chains. He would have been only a slave, pure and happy perhaps, but still a slave."

"He would have been better off to have been a slave, or never to have been born, rather than run the risk of eternal damnation."

"Blasphemy! The peril that we are in, the struggle that we have to make against it, is what gives our life its grandeur. Without struggle there is no merit. Without free will, without temptations to be overcome, we would have no more character than a stone that falls or an insect that flies."

81

"Father, you say that because you feel you are certain of salvation, but are you thinking of others?"

"I beg your pardon; I am not at all certain of salvation. As a priest, I bear a responsibility which is heavy indeed in proportion to my weakness. And as for the unregenerate and the wicked, I never cease to think of them. How could I, when I am offering my life for them, and when I have no other object but to enlighten them and help them? To my mind," he added gently, "that is a higher charity than wishing to lose oneself with them."

But Adélaide remained troubled and unconvinced.

"Michel," she said when she had found her husband, "if I should lose my soul, if I should be cut off from the Church because I refused to believe in hell and you were certain that I was damned, could you resign yourself to it?"

He pressed her close to him.

"I could never believe that a soul like yours was lost. Love, if nothing else, would lead you to the light. But the Church is a surer guide. We must not reject its teachings, for our reason often shows us how incontestable they are, even when our hearts rebel against them. One does not deny a fact because it saddens him. The dogma of original sin is only the affirmation of a fact. The Church teaches us that the whole race is subject to the heredity of the first man. Science confirms that teaching. I can verify in my own patients that syphilitics and alcoholics transmit their physiological defects to their children. It is a law which we cannot deny. In the same way, man who fell, who became mortal, transmitted death to his descendants. But God, who is love, drew our greatest blessing from our adversity. He came down to earth incarnate. And the Cross has restored to us a heaven more beautiful than the paradise which we lost."

This time also, her objections fell from her. Whereas she rebelled against Father Athanase's teachings, she received Michel's humbly, even eagerly. For while he used the same arguments as the monk, his emphasis was wholly different. The problems which his friend found simple, still troubled Michel profoundly even though he accepted the Catholic solution. He was still saddened by the mystery of the world. As a new convert, he remembered the weight of anxiety and doubt which he had carried. Despite his faith, he understood error and his heart went out to it. Their walks became long meditations in which Michel, in struggling to resolve his own difficulties, struggled to resolve those of his companion also.

"You doubt, Adé," he said, "and you accuse God of cruelty, but if you reject God, the cruelty becomes more cruel and more inexplicable still. Just as you, I am often tempted to rebel against suffering, but I take refuge in the Church which alone gives the world significance and enables us to accept it.

"We must realize," he added, "that we have a long

road to travel, an immense purification to undergo before we can recapture the Christian state of mind in its entirety. Perhaps we have not sinned greatly, but the spirit of the world is in us and corrupts our judgments. Our opinions on the gravest subjects are still superficial. We give too much importance to pain, not enough to sin. As a result of having associated constantly with people for whom God does not exist, whose souls are, as it were, paralyzed, and who act only according to the dictates of their appetites and passions, we have come to look with abject complacency on the gravest faults. What is adultery to us, sensuality, falsehood, fraud, the mad desire for luxury and pleasure? Nothing, less than nothing. God keep us from ever being disdainful toward a sinner, but sin is a wholly tragic thing which we must look upon with horror. It should wound us as ugliness does, stifle us like a nauseous odor. Evil exists and from it springs all the suffering of the world. We must take arms against it. The monks, the priests, all the clergy have understood that thoroughly. They alone possess a sense of true charity. They are the warriors of Christ, an army few in numbers but which is battling step by step to defend the weak and the foolish and the indifferent against the forces of darkness."

One day, at noon, as they were walking together beside a field where some lay brothers were engaged in taking in the hay, the angelus sounded. Their faces suddenly alight, their hands clasped, the men slipped from the world of toil into the world of meditation. Looking at those homely figures, whose souls shone so brilliantly, Michel stopped in awe.

"There is one thing of which I am sure, absolutely sure," he said; "that is that those men are in the way of truth. Humble as they are, toil-worn, and with no time for repose except in prayer, they are greater than the sages and the philosophers. Sometimes I would like to drop on my knees before them."

There was such fervor in his voice that Adélaide felt a sudden fear.

"Need one admire them so much?" she said coldly. "They already have their reward since, as Father Athanase says, they are so perfectly happy."

"A happiness which is based on abnegation and renunciation. It is the only perfect happiness. All other is less beautiful."

The cruel words which seemed to condemn their lives and their love stabbed at her heart. She had the impression that her husband was escaping her. She felt mysterious aspirations in him with which she had no concern. The threat which was hanging over her happiness was growing greater, and she did not know how to defend herself. The thought came to her that Father Athanase might help her. By chance, the next day Michel went to Dinant, and she met the monk in the woods beside the abbey. He was disengaged and willingly granted her the interview she requested. A hundred yards from the cloister, under a great oak, there was a bench where the brothers sometimes came to read or meditate. The two sat down there. Through a thin curtain of trees they could look out over the valley. It was a dazzling day and the green of the leaves and grass contrasted in almost blinding vividness with the blue of the sky. But Adélaide paid no attention to the scene.

"Father," she said, "today I would like to talk to you not of myself but of Michel." She added with a trace of bitterness: "You know him now better than I."

He bent his head without reply, for he had a horror of futile discussion. Seeing that he would not help her, she went on:

"I have been noticing for some time that he has seemed changed. I don't feel that I wholly understand him any more. He wounded me cruelly yesterday. . . ."

She stopped in embarrassment. Her eyes were full of tears. The monk was still silent. He attached no importance to women's petty grievances and sentimentalities. She realized that to interest him she must express herself more precisely.

"As Michel's director," she said, "don't you feel that his exaltation is excessive?"

Father Athanase knew how quickly she could experience a change of heart. He thought that her

86

fervor was already slackening at contact with a faith stronger and more burning than her own.

"I see no trace of exaltation in Michel," he said firmly. "Every truly generous spirit—and his is of that number—when it gives itself, gives itself without reservation. God is no beggar, asking for a piece of the soul, no matter how small, how mediocre. He requires it all."

"But," she continued almost desperately, "God does not ask the same of everyone. That He should ask everything of you, whom He has chosen for His priest is perfectly normal. But those who are not called to the priesthood have human duties and affections which God surely cannot require them to sacrifice."

This time the monk nodded his head in assent. She went on, encouraged:

"So what does my husband's attitude signify? Why is he so indifferent to everything that used to constitute his life? Why does he give so little thought to his career, to me? Why does he have to go so high, so far? I cannot follow him. One would think our happiness seemed wicked to him. One would think that apart from religion and things eternal, nothing here on earth had any value for him any more."

Michel is simple and straightforward and extraordinarily intense," said Dom Athanase slowly after reflection. "He has always felt the need of immersing himself in a great task, of devoting himself to a great idea. For a long time he served science with the zeal of an apostle, and science betrayed him. He saw that it was incapable of bringing peace to the earth. The war overturned, destroyed, everything in which he had believed. He was left without hope, truly bereft, alone. . . ."

"Alone," thought Adélaide. "And yet I was with him, I whom he says he loves."

"Then God, by a prodigy of His infinite mercy revealed Himself to him in his want," went on the monk. "Almost without transition, Michel has passed from dearth to abundance, from ignorance to certainty. He has found at last that which he has always been seeking: absolute truth, perfect beauty, the Being who cannot disappoint. He is dazzled by the light to such an extent that he sees only it and not that which it illumines. At the same time, he is overwhelmed by a feeling of the glory of God. Having received, unasked, the greatest of graces, he wishes to respond magnificently, unstintingly. That is the cause of his disdain for happiness, his desire for immolation, his intangible aspirations. If his conversion had taken place ten years earlier, doubtless he would have entered a cloister."

Not for a moment did the monk sense Adélaide's jealousy. She had asked a question and he was answering it in all frankness, explaining his friend's state of mind as he interpreted it. Cut off from the world, he had no conception of the insane demands which love makes, he had no idea that this tortured woman who was listening to him looked upon God as her rival in Michel's heart. But she, hoping for comfort, was transfixed by his words. Suddenly she attributed to him a Machiavellian scheme: he was trying to separate her from Michel, to destroy their love. That was why he was always enticing his friend to the abbey. He was picturing the ecclesiastical life to him as the only ideal worthy of a noble spirit. At last she thought she understood the danger that was threatening her and with her eyes blazing she hurled her defiance at the monk.

"You shan't take him from me!"

Father Athanase could only express his immense surprise in his expression. She gave him no chance to speak, her words came in a torrent.

"I won't let you. Whatever you are trying to do, whatever you think about Michel, stop! You can't go on. He is mine. He married me, not the Church. On earth and in heaven I come first. He married me before men and before God. I have a right to him. Whatever you do, everything is on my side: law, the sacraments, society, the Pope. No, you shan't take him from me!"

Her voice, high and strident at first, broke on the last words, trailed off into a sob. The monk let her cry for a few moments to exhaust some of her senseless fury. Her anguish moved him deeply. He loved joy, he saw it manifest in everything about him and he never ceased to be astonished that so many people should refuse that which was freely offered. When Adélaide seemed more calm, he swept his arm toward the trees, the sky, the fields, all the smiling things which surrounded them.

"Look," he said with a heartiness mingled with compassion, "look around you. This wood might be a symbol of your own life: tranquil, sheltered, with beauty wherever you turn. You have but to thank God and enjoy his blessings. Why do you torment yourself so, inventing imaginary dangers? Why defend yourself so fiercely when nothing threatens you? You completely distort the meaning of my words. When I say that Michel, if he had been free, would doubtless have entered a cloister, it is a simple supposition of no importance. It in no way signifies that I would like to see him there. Quite the contrary. His place is in the world. He has duties there which he will worthily perform as soon as he, as well as you, understands how human love and the love of God go hand in hand. I am here to help you both. You make a mistake if you feel that you have anything to fear from me. The matrimonial bond is a sacred bond in my eyes, as it is in the eyes of every priest. It can be broken in only one case."

"What is that?" she asked, a little ashamed of her vehemence, but still apprehensive.

"It is not a case that will concern you, so have no fear," he said, smiling. "It could only be if you and

Michel both were called to the Church. Then mutual consent could free you of your vows. I recently saw a husband and wife, an admirable couple, renounce each other for obligations higher than those of marriage. They separated with the permission of the Holy Father, and entered the cloister. I scarcely believe you will be tempted to follow their example."

She drew a deep breath. The air seemed suddenly divinely pure.

"No," she said, "you are quite right. I have put all my happiness in a single person. Neither my ambition nor my desires go beyond him. He is sufficient for me, for always."

"Then keep him, Madame," concluded the priest, "and make him as happy as you can, loving him in God as he loves you. And have no more fear of me. I am not your enemy."

He held out his hand with a frank smile, and moved away. Adélaide sat where she was, a sensation of peace mounting within her. Above her the branches, swaying in the wind, parted now and then to let shafts of sunlight through. The leaves and the grass gleamed in the brightness, then fell back into shadow. The heaviness of mid-day brought a sort of sweet torpor. She was deliciously reassured, she felt that her great treasure had now been won back and that she never would let it escape again.

VI.

AS Adélaide thought about Father Athanase's words—"Then keep him, Madame, and make him as happy as you can"—they took on ironic overtones. The simple admonition threw into relief the ever increasing limitations of her influence over Michel. He no longer sought his happiness in her and she could give him nothing for which he really thirsted. Never had he shown her more consistent, more solicitous, or more meaningless tenderness. "Loving her in God" seemed to him to mean loving her as a sister, loving her as he did his fellow man, as he did a perfect stranger. She, on the other hand, loved her husband with all her body as well as with her soul, and she wanted to be loved similarly in return. Since the first days of their stay in Evolayne, he had rarely come to knock on her door in the evening. And since her conversion, he had limited himself to bestowing a calm, fraternal kiss upon her each morning and evening which drove her to despair. She tried in vain to make him aware of her beauty once more. Never, with a flattering word, did he confirm what her mirror told her. Never again did he tremble at the loveliness of her face as he had that evening when he had said: "Don't be so beauti-ful." Frequently, he criticized her dresses and said they were indecent. He complained of the strength of her perfumes. She was at a loss to understand.

"Does he think it is a sin to love me?" she asked herself. "After all, I am his wife. The Church per-mits love between a husband and wife."

She would have died rather than confess her shame-ful secret. Nevertheless someone had guessed it. Two days after her interview with Father Athanase, Michel spent the night at her side. A bitter night during which, long after he was asleep, she lay weeping in the dark. Never had she felt more lonely than in his arms. She was all but certain that he had come to her solely out of duty, probably at the direct command of the monk. Nor was she mistaken. In her passion-ate outpouring, Dom Athanase had recognized the importunities of a woman abandoned by her lover. Long experience as a confessor had taught him to be alert to such danger signals. In his eyes, and in the eyes of the Church, Michel was incurring grave responsibilities in neglecting a young and ardent wife. Sooner or later, his indifference might have disastrous consequences. The monk questioned his friend and reminded him that a married man was not required to live in perfect chastity, that on the contrary he should fulfill his marital obligations and not relinquish the hope of issue. Such interven-tion was odious to Adélaide. She wanted to be loved freely and not in obedience to the laws of marriage. Thenceforth it was she who kept Michel at a distance. Every evening when she said good night, she complained of being tired and locked her door ostentatiously behind her. She loved him so much that she was willing to share his ascetic ideal. Little by little, her privation became a source of delight for her. Her love, no longer finding its normal outlet, became exalted, drew its satisfaction from the slightest things. Michel became a stranger to her again. Once more, at the mere feeling of his physical presence, emotions stirred in her which habit had long since caused her to forget. The touch of his hand sent as much rapture through her now as his most burning kisses had done before. His nearness, his glance, his smile satisfied her because she was starving. She might, eventually, have been happy in this renunciation of all physical union if only their spiritual accord had been complete. She tried every day to make it more perfect. Submissively she attended all the offices with Michel, received communion with him, strove to merge herself with him in God. But his soul escaped her, even as they prayed side by side, for as she was thinking only of him, he was oblivious of her. His only reading now was the literature of theology which she did not understand. Formerly, when he was tired of the cold realities of science, he had turned to art, to beauty, to poetry, to love, for the surge of the spirit which sweeps the soul up to heights made of heroic dreams and infinite desires. Now books and his wife seemed a paltry world to him. God's limitless, dazzling universe opened before his impatient, ever-questing spirit, and he felt that he was living only when he was at the abbey.

Out of condescension, however, he sometimes accompanied Adélaide on her walks. Even as he paced at her side she felt him far off, distracted, absorbed in religious meditations. For a few days, a spell of scorching heat forced them to forego their excursions. Then a storm broke. Shortly after, they set out in the soft, warm, perfume-laden air. The path they chose was a narrow, winding one through the woods. Thickets hemmed them in on either side and Adélaide pressed forward joyfully, parting the rain-soaked branches. Anyone might have taken delight in watching her high spirits, so graceful were her movements, so supple her body as she bounded and twisted like a young animal. But Michel seemed to disapprove, to consider indecorous such Bacchic exuberance over the fresh greenness of the forest. At length he lost her to sight and sat down to wait. Soon she came running back wreathed about with honeysuckle. From waist to shoulder, she was covered with the flowers and the green leaves. She held out her bare, dew-covered arms toward him.

"How old are you anyway, Adé?" he asked morosely.

She stopped still, put a hand on his breast and

95

looked at him with an expression of sad interrogation.

"And you, Michel, how old are you? How many centuries? Doesn't your heart still beat? Can't anything please you any more?"

He stood up, shrugging his shoulders.

"Do you expect me to lose my head just because a storm has made the forest more beautiful than usual? Do you think I'm going to join you in your wild, pagan, voluptuous worship of nature?"

"But what harm is there in it?" she asked softly. "O, Michel, you have lost all sense of what is innocent. The woods are innocent, my play was innocent. But to you everything is impure now, everything is tainted: nature, and poetry, and flowers, and your wife. Am I truly so wicked, such a burden to you?"

She unwound the honeysuckle and held it out to him with a timid smile. He took it, then let it drop.

"Please go back," she said in a low, restrained voice.

"Why?" he asked, annoyed but patient. "Let us go on with our walk."

"Go back!" she cried, losing control, "leave me to myself. It stifles me to be with you. I am no nun. I am a living woman. I love the leaves and the trees and the water. There is nothing sinful in this forest, there is nothing good or evil about the trees. I want to gather flowers, I want to . . ."

She did not finish but turned and fled, so quickly that he made no attempt to follow her.

It was true that she was stifling. Whereas Michel, by his conversion, had cut himself off from all else, she remained faithful to that which she had loved. Religion, as her husband understood it, was tyranny to a soul such as hers, made to vibrate with all the human emotions. In a sudden revulsion of feeling, the abbey and prayers wearied her to desperation. She longed for the most frivolous pleasures. The cafés of Paris, the theaters, the ballrooms, the stores seemed the acme of delight. She scorned herself for wanting to go back to them so much.

"We have lost our sense of balance, going so quickly from a worldly life to a religious one," she said to herself, clutching at justification. "Little by little, things will take on their proper values after we have gotten away from here. We can continue to be Christians but just the same we shall be able to live."

She was desperately anxious to leave. They had been at Evolayne for three months. It was now almost the end of September. Michel, rested by such a long holiday, was in condition to go back to his work. She summoned her courage to speak to him about it. The suggestion upset him more than she had anticipated.

"I was thinking," he stammered, "that we might stay on until the end of October. Father Athanase says the fall is beautiful here and you love that season so."

.She was not taken in by so obvious a ruse. And when he added, almost timidly: "After all, there is nothing calling us back," she interposed firmly:

"What about your patients?"

"I have written to my substitute," he confessed with growing embarrassment. "He is willing to fill in for me as long as I wish. I have every confidence in him."

"Take care that he doesn't take your practice away from you permanently."

He did not understand, or pretended not to understand, her meaning.

"Are you so in need of money that the loss of a few patients seems an irremediable disaster to you?"

"It is not a question of money," she flashed, wounded that he could ascribe such a motive to her. "I was only thinking of you. I want you to have a fine, interesting career. And you will jeopardize it by staying away too long. A man is quickly forgotten in Paris. If your patients fall into the habit of going to other doctors, you will be idle and bored."

Logical as was her reasoning, he seemed unmoved. He sighed as if she were being willfully obtuse.

"Michel," she said sadly, "you don't care about your profession any more. Why don't you admit it?"

"It does seem less noble and necessary to me than it once did. Any man, provided he makes a serious study of it, can cure, or at least relieve, bodily suffering. But for the greater mission, the saving of souls, there are few workers."

She remembered Father Athanase's words and she asked him, her voice taut:

"Do you think, then, you have chosen the wrong career?"

"How can I know?" he said reflectively. "Certainly I would have done better if I had taken a professorship. There, one can exercise an influence upon young people, show them how to lead Christian lives."

Reassured by his uncertainty, she made herself gentle, persuasive.

"You would have made an inspiring teacher, there is no question about it. But it seems to me that there is an immense field of activity open to you in the work you have chosen, and which you are now disdaining. Who are more willing to listen than the sick, particularly to the man who is taking care of them? If he wishes, a doctor can so easily become their friend, their confidant. They are grateful for his every attention and they will listen to his advice with respect. Through the body he can wield an enormous power over the soul, he can comfort it and guide it. It seems to me his rôle is very close to that of the priest."

"That is very much what Father Athanase was saying to me," said Michel approvingly, half-convinced.

"You are a charming preacher, Adé. I shall try to be worthy of my rôle of a Christian physician."

However, events favored his secret desire. The very next day he learned that a great ceremony was to be held at Evolayne at the end of October, in which four young monks were to be received into the priesthood. Adélaide willingly consented to postpone their departure for she too was eager, once in her life, to witness an ordination.

In the great city cathedrals, the enormous crowd which such a ceremony always draws detracts from its impressiveness. But at Evolayne, it was clothed in extraordinary pomp and solemnity. Though the sixty-six ecclesiastics who participated were imposing in their numbers, there was but a sparse lay attendance. The pilgrims who all summer had been thronging to the monastery, were few now that the bad weather was approaching. The villagers, devout as they were, took little interest in the austere rite of ordination. Only the families who were that day giving their sons to the Lord, had come from far off to be present at their sacrifice.

The Bishop of Namur officiated. Shortly before the gospel, he interrupted the Mass. The candidates for ordination, their chasubles folded over their left arms, knelt around him. In her book, Adélaide followed the short dialogue which ensued between the archdeacon and the prelate:

Most Reverend Father, our Holy Mother, the

Catholic Church, asks that you ordain these deacons here present, to the office of the priesthood.

Do you know them to be worthy?

As far as human frailty allows, I do know and bear witness that they are worthy of the charge of this office.

The bishop gave thanks to God. Then in a resonant voice he adjured the clergy and the people to speak their mind, if necessary, so that he might not entrust the divine mission to souls that were unworthy. Addressing the future priests, he reminded them of the obligations inherent in their ministry, and the responsibilities that they were about to assume forever. Before conferring so awful a dignity upon them, he warned them against all weaknesses of the flesh and spirit. This moment was still given to them to weigh their souls in the balance before advancing to the altar to renew the mystery of the death of Christ. The celebration of that sacrament demanded the renunciation of all concupiscence and all earthly attachment, and the prelate, paternal and severe, halted his children on the brink of immolation and, for the last time, issued the warning:

Ponder well the step you are about to take, so that the Lord may neither condemn us for elevating you to so high an office, nor you for not maintaining yourselves in it.

How solemn this moment, in which these young deacons stood, still free, but face to face with their austere, sublime destiny. The strongest of them might well have trembled, but fortified by humility they were unshaken, however conscious of their immense frailty. Grace alone, which they would receive with ordination, would confer the necessary holiness upon them. It was sufficient for them to offer themselves in faith and fervor, and to reply to the Master's call with loving eagerness. Unhesitatingly, fearlessly, they prostrated themselves simultaneously at the foot of the altar, in token of their death to the world. And as they lay prostrate, motionless forms patiently submitting to the divine power operating upon their souls, the choir intoned the Litany of the Saints, and continued the alternate chants until interrupted by the three invocations prescribed for the bishop:

That Thou wouldst vouchsafe to bless these chosen ones,

That Thou wouldst vouchsafe to bless and sanctify these chosen ones,

That Thou wouldst vouchsafe to bless and sanctify and consecrate these chosen ones,

We beseech Thee, hear us!

Then the chant ceased and perfect stillness reigned. The four prostrate figures rose to a kneeling posture and the bishop imposed his hands upon them. Then all the monks, leaving their stalls, came one by one to perform the same rite. After they had filed past, they grouped themselves about the young deacons and, extending their right arms in an august gesture, held their consecrated hands over the heads of the candidates. They remained for some moments, motionless. Surrounded by that dark assemblage, none could see the four kneeling forms. It was as though the living church were closing in upon its captives. That circle of monks about them, that crown of hands above their heads represented the spiritual cloister which, more than the walls and grilles of the monastery, already separated them from the world. The awful charge of priesthood, its wisdom, its rigor, its premature old age, was descending upon those young elect whom the bishop was about to make priests forever.

It was at that moment that Adélaide, overwhelmed by the majesty of what she was witnessing, looked about in the audience for her husband, hoping to catch his eye to share her impressions with him. During these solemn ceremonies, the men were separated from the women and were placed on the right side of the nave. Michel was standing a little behind her, at the end of a row. Turning, she saw him almost full face, with the light shining on him. He was not looking for her, he was not thinking of her. His eyes were riveted on the choir, on the group of monks standing rigid in their hieratic attitude. The muscles of his face were taut and his mouth trembled slightly. The extraordinary intensity of his gaze was as eloquent as a cry. Through it, his soul, imprisoned, was reaching out in desperate longing toward that which was forbidden, inaccessible to him. And his face, caught thus unaware, betrayed such infinite regret, such infinite yearning that the comprehension suddenly swept over Adélaide of how total was the disaster of their two lives. Michel's happiness was there at the altar; he knew it, and he knew that his dream would never come to pass. He was bitterly envying those privileged ones whom the Church was taking to herself. He was suffering that he could not follow them. At the sight of his so obvious pain, Adélaide forgot her own. She had dropped to her knees and she prayed, sobbingly:

"O Lord, if, when I was still so much a part of the world and unmindful of Thy laws, I had seen him, my husband, fall in love with another woman, I should have set him free. Now since it is for Thee only that he yearns, must I be a chain forever keeping him from Thee? Because he once loved me with a fleeting love, not knowing that his love could find fulfillment only in Thee, can he not give himself as he desires, can he not take Thy Church as his spouse? Since Thou wilt not permit him to abandon me, then at least deliver him of me, grant me death or . . ."

A sudden thought pierced through her. She remembered the man and wife about whom Father Athanase had spoken, who had separated to enter the cloister.

"Why," she thought, "shouldn't we receive the same grace? O Lord, couldst Thou not call me now? Choose me, so that Michel may have the right to choose Thee. Dear God, Thou knowest that I love Thee, even though it be less than I love him. Destroy his image in me, obliterate it and replace it with Thine own. I offer myself to Thee, humbly. Thou knowest that everything which my own desire and will can do, I have tried. But it is Thou alone who must give the vocation; render me worthy to obtain it."

She prayed thus for a long time, her face hidden in her hands, not conscious of what was going on about her. Then her mounting grief became too heavy for her to bear alone. As a Catholic, she was not without intercessors before God. Secretly, she transferred her burden to the young deacons who were being ordained, imploring them to plead for her. Surely, that day their prayers would be all-powerful. Nor had she any doubt that they were taking upon themselves all the aspirations, all the suffering, of the faithful who were present. She felt a tenderness in the thought that, without knowing her, they were nevertheless praying for her as she had prayed for them. She raised her head and looked at them.

They were standing at the foot of the altar in the fullness of their new dignity. The words of consecration had passed over them, marking them with an indelible sign which on earth, in heaven, nay, even in hell should they fall from grace, would indicate to everyone, eternally, that they were priests. They had been clothed with their priestly vestments, the stole and the chasuble. With their bound hands they had touched the chalice, and the paten, and the host. They now possessed the power to offer to God the Holy Sacrifice. Even now, in a sense, they were celebrating what was really their first Mass, as they recited with the bishop the liturgical prayers. And if, shortly before, they had trembled at the awfulness of their future task, they could not find reassurance, for the words of Jesus Christ, which had been so severe, now became infinitely tender. The prelate, having given them communion, was intoning from the right hand side of the altar, the hymn of friendship:

I will not call you servants
But "my friends"
For now you know all things
Whatsoever I have wrought
In your midst

Receive in you the Holy Ghost,
The Consoler;
He it is,
Whom the Father will send to you.

Then indeed will you be my friends,
If you do the things
That I have commanded you.

Again Adélaide turned toward her husband. He
had not, as she had, lost half the ceremony. He had
been following intently every detail of the rite, and
as he had done so, a blessed illusion had taken possession of him. He had identified himself with the
newly ordained priests, had prayed and trembled
and triumphed with them. Now, in the belief that
he was one of them, he was taking to himself
that hymn of friendship. His face had relaxed,
his eyes were shining with the ecstasy of deliverance.

Soon, however, something warned him that he was
being observed. His eyes left the altar, roved uncertainly, dazedly, then encountered Adélaide's. At that,
slowly, the dream in which he had just been living
began to fade. He was not a priest, not one of these
elect crowned by God's favor; he was a man as other
men, who, when he was free to aspire to all the delights of life in God, had chosen, had preferred, this
woman. She was his, indissolubly, forever. He possessed nothing but her, this wife so beautiful and so
imperfect, this creature of clay, in place of the Infinite Being. And each looked at the other with the
same poignancy and the same sadness. Each reproached the other in silence.

"You deceived me," said Michel. "You are not happiness."

"I would have been happiness if you had loved me," said Adélaide. "Woman exists only through love, and your faithlessness has robbed me of everything."

The ceremony came to an end and they went out together. By mutual consent they turned into the wood near the abbey. The bench under the oak invited them and they sat down. The silence was unbroken. Through the trembling fretwork of leaves, the valley shone like a gulf of sunlight. Adélaide, her eyes half-closed, leaned on her husband's shoulder. She felt no rancor against him. She understood and reverenced the new love that was burning in that heart where she once had reigned. She accepted being dispossessed.

"Michel, I feel all unstrung," she murmured plaintively. "It was so beautiful, too beautiful! . . . I have seen the greatest of human dreams realized. Those new priests . . . think of their happiness . . . the hour that they have just lived! . . . Everything pales beside it. . . . It's true that the world offers nothing to compare with it."

She could hardly finish her sentences. Her lips were parted and she struggled for breath as if she were ill.

"How can one help envying them!" said Michel fervently. "What a recompense is theirs already, in exchange for so slight a sacrifice. No longer God's servants, but his friends! His friends! . . . The All-Powerful admits, invites that unending intimacy. He doesn't wish to be the master, He makes Himself the equal of His poor children. The whole solemn, yes, awful, ceremony ends with that tenderness, in that overwhelming affirmation of His love."

Without looking at him, with her head on his breast as if to catch the slightest quickening of his heart, Adélaide asked:

"Michel, if I should die, you would become a priest, wouldn't you?"

He hesitated a moment, sensing the trap.

"If you should die," he said gently, "there could be no consolation for me except in God."

His reply, calculated as it was, was significant to Adélaide. If he had been truly in love with her, would he not have refused to think of her death, or would he not have denied that it would be possible to go on living, having lost her? But for him, now, no trial held any terrors. He was utterly confident in the support of the One who could not die, who could never fail him. And, bitterly, Adélaide acknowledged to herself that he was wise in giving himself to no finite being, for she foresaw with what suffering she would pay for her love for him. Never before had grief to such an extent overwhelmed her. In an endeavor to deaden its pain, after luncheon she set out, as she so often did, for a walk. She plunged into the woods, and cutting through them, came out into the vast, all but treeless plain on the other side. It was a burning Indian summer afternoon, hot in the mid-day sun as the most scorching days of summer. For a long time she plodded on in the blazing heat, trying to add weariness to weariness. She returned at sunset, her head on fire, her body shaken by chills. She was forced to take to her bed. Michel nursed her solicitously. On the third day, her fever fell.

"You can get up now," he told her. "Your foolhardy expeditions gave you a touch of sunstroke. Be more prudent the next time."

She had thought that she was fatally ill and she was incredulous at being told she was well again. If that were the case, what was the cause of this change in her, this sudden feeling of old age, this indifference about everything which had concerned her heretofore? Books lay on her table unopened. The presence or absence of Michel caused her neither pleasure nor pain. She did not care whether she went back to Paris. It was a matter of no concern to her where she was. If this sensation of detachment were not caused by illness, by the approach of death, might it not be the mark of the inward transforming process of grace? The truth was that the certainty of no longer being loved had alone laid waste her soul, had withered all that once flourished there. But she did not understand that. She believed that in answer to her prayer, God was emptying her heart of all else in order that He might establish Himself there.

One evening when she had gone to bed early and Michel was sitting beside her, reading, she asked suddenly, dreamily:

"Did Dom Athanase tell you about the man and wife who renounced each other so that they could give themselves entirely to God?"

Michel looked up with interest and closed his book willingly.

"Yes," he said, "I know the story well. They were converted by Father Athanase's brother, a Dominican, at a time when he was in Paris, preaching a retreat. What miracle of grace could it have been that led those two unbelievers who never went to church, to listen to the urging of a devout friend of theirs and go to those services that one evening in Lent? Grief had opened the way for them. They had just lost a little girl, their only child, and they could find no comfort in anything. That night the preacher was expounding the parable of the daughter of Jairus, and was explaining Christ's words: 'The child is not dead, she is sleeping.' They listened. Their hearts were touched. The ordinary practices of religion, which they resumed, proved insufficient for them. Both wished to sacrifice their entire lives."

"How beautiful," murmured Adélaide. "But you said grief had opened the way by cutting them off from every other interest. They offered broken hearts . . ."

She reflected a moment and went on in a voice at once timid and fervent:

"How much more beautiful it would be to offer a heart that was happy, to go to God not seeking consolation, but bringing it."

Michel was astonished at the loftiness of her words. Not for a long time had he looked at Adélaide with such tenderness. Was this a disinterested, objective opinion that she was expressing, or might it be a cry straight from her soul, her deepest wish? She did not leave him long in doubt. She went on, fixing him with her eyes.

"The cloister attracts you, Michel, you can't deny it. It is not without attraction to me."

The words saw him suddenly transfigured. The faintly sad serenity he had worn like a mask over his face was torn aside by a wild burst of joy. His blood raced and he trembled at the possibility of a happiness which he had thought unattainable. To Adélaide's great surprise, his emotion, the significance of which she understood perfectly, troubled her very little. There was a slight tightening in her heart, then again she felt at peace.

"It is only a question of allowing grace to act," she thought. "Its power is irresistible. Already, God alone reigns in me as he does in Michel."

"Who knows," she said with a tranquil smile, "but

that we have been chosen to follow and surpass their great example, for we were happy in each other, Michel; you were wholly sufficient to me. How does it happen that I too am tempted to renounce you?"

He leaned toward her, his face pale and his eyes shining.

"Can it be true?" he stammered. "O, let us pray ardently, let us ask the father to pray for us. If you have heard the call of God as I have, let us answer it joyously, let us show ourselves worthy!"

When Michel repeated Adélaide's words to Dom Athanase, the latter refused flatly to attach the least importance to them. His mind concerning his penitent was made up. He recognized qualities in her which he greatly esteemed. With her, no one need fear hypocrisy or subterfuge. She was straightforward, loyal, sincere even in her changes of heart, but immeasurably weak. By the criteria of the world, hers was an exemplary soul. But in the eyes of the priest it was weak because it was wholly under the sway of passion. Fortunately, the love which dominated her was entirely licit. But she would have surrendered to it just as unreservedly if it had been otherwise. Far from having any innate concept of duty, she called "good" that toward which her heart impelled her. Like the poets, she built a world after her own pattern. She had a certain sense of the heroic, she admired self-sacrifice, and as a result she was apt to become exalted, to dream of great actions which she was incapable of carrying out. The monk smilingly accused his friend of having taken over-seriously the mystic transports induced by the grandeur of the ordination ceremony.

"If you had heard her, Father," insisted Michel, "you wouldn't have any doubt. God has touched her as He did me. Some great change is being wrought within her."

The monk put his hand on Michel's shoulder and looked deep and commandingly into his eyes.

"Dear friend," he said, "if God has some exceptional purpose regarding you, He will reveal it to us at the proper time. But recent converts are often misled by an excess of zeal. They are apt to believe they have been called to make acts of extraordinary self-abnegation. For myself, I have no other ambition than to see you fulfill simply and devotedly the duties you have already assumed. Be humble, be calm, be like a little child who walks with his hand in his father's hand, not asking whither he is going. It seems to me that the time has come for you to go back to Paris."

VII.

DESPITE the temporary shattering of his hopes, Michel recognized the wisdom of the priest's words and, after reflection, he determined to obey him scrupulously, yet not to close his mind to aspiration. He submitted to the counsel he had received with the calm decision of those who, filled with a great ideal, are willing to fight and suffer to bring it to pass. The thought of returning to Paris no longer dispirited him; he looked upon it now as a test of faith. There was a hope within him which gave him strength.

Before saying farewell to his two penitents, Father Athanase received them several more times and talked at length with one after the other. He exhorted them primarily to show themselves faithful in little things and made no allusion to the possibility of a double vocation. Adélaide was somewhat surprised, but Michel understood and approved.

"The priest's rôle is essentially that of a moderator," he explained to her. "His mission is to resist good as well as evil. He holds back the weak when they are tempted, and he also holds back the presumptuous who wish to conquer the kingdom of God too quickly. That is where our director, very wisely, has become our adversary. He knows what we both are hoping, but he refuses to listen to us; he resists and waits in silence. It is well that it should be so. It is for us to persevere. Doubtless we shall have to knock for a long time at the door of the temple before it is opened to us. But we shall know how to be patient."

The words his wife had spoken were rarely out of Michel's mind. It seemed to him almost a miracle that at the moment when he was trying to stifle the hopes which he thought never could be realized, his wife, for whom he was sacrificing them, should have formulated a wish similar to his own. That unexpected remark changed the course of their lives. For Adélaide saw that he still had faith in her.

The atmosphere of Paris in no way weakened their belief. The cloister which meditation throws around fervent souls, stood undiminished about them. Though they were in the world, they were not of it. They received no visitors, they saw only each other. Michel took care that none of the graces received at Evolayne should be forgotten. Devoured by his desire to spread the Gospel, he very naturally found in his wife his first disciple. The malleable soul which in the young girl he had modeled for himself, he now re-fashioned, transforming it that it might be given to God.

She submitted to a spiritual possession so much

more absolute than physical possession that she all but lost the power of thinking for herself. Michel's strong, zealous, unswerving will imposed itself upon her own, which, eager though it was, tired quickly. Both now studied the word of God as once they had studied the poets. Adélaide, oversensitive to the beauties of the visible world, found the splendors of the invisible nearly impossible to picture. Michel explained them to her. He revealed the whole of his ardor to her, overwhelming her with the intensity of his faith. Unresisting, she let herself be destroyed and built up again by him.

She confessed, briefly, to various priests in her parish, none of whom knew her, but in reality Michel was her director. To be with him, and to please him, she began to attend daily communion. The necessity of rising early in the morning made it impossible for them to go out in the evening or to attend any social functions. She had no other distraction than her profane books. Michel asked the sacrifice of them. In his zeal as a neophyte, he now renounced everything which he had most loved. The greatest masterpieces troubled his jealous orthodoxy. Genius he accounted nothing, since his discovery of holiness. Adélaide defended the poets. For her they remained sacred beings, inspired by God, irrespective of their religious doctrines.

"Don't condemn those who can spread such enchantment," she pleaded. "I owe everything that was good and noble in my soul before my conversion to them. It was due to them that, even without religion, I kept a taste for the beautiful and the eternal."

"Perhaps that was true for me also. Their task was to keep the spiritual flame burning. But useful as their words may be to pagans and atheists and materialists, for Christians they are not only empty, but actually harmful. With the exception of the poets who submit to the authority of the Church, they all, inevitably, fall into strange idolatries: nature, humanity, progress, love. Those are the false Gods they offer us. You must realize, Adélaide, that truth admits no rivalry. We cannot give either our admiration or our friendship to those who glorify error. That is why you have seen me put away forever so many books which were once dear to me. What I have done, can't you do also?"

When he spoke to her like that, with that look of supplication and confidence, she felt herself capable of any renunciation, fearing only to disappoint him. Besides, the forces so fiercely repressed within her were palpitant to spend themselves in sacrifice. Her love, ministered to no longer, could find release only in giving. She stripped herself of everything that was precious to her, she no longer opened the books which had nourished her spirit, she forbade herself all regret for the past, all escape into the future. She ceased to be dreamy and impulsive. The Church was her refuge, prayer her constant occupation, liturgy her study, the sacred texts the only poetry permitted. Michel marveled to see her so changed. One day he exclaimed in pride and tenderness:

"I was not mistaken about your soul. It was made for the sublime."

She hid her face on his shoulder.

"I owe everything to you. You are my creator."

He was startled at her idolatry and reproved her sternly:

"Do not confound me with God. He alone created you and offers you salvation. The transformation taking place in you is not the result of any human agency."

She acknowledged her fault instantly, reproached herself for having given way so unrestrainedly to her feelings. Thenceforth she struggled against her tenderness, renounced the most innocent familiarities. She no longer allowed her hand to rest in his for more than a moment. She marveled that she suffered less than she had anticipated. The emotions of her daily, difficult renunciation not only replaced those of the love she no longer permitted herself, but surpassed them both in intensity and exquisiteness. The anguish of their prospective separation gave infinite value to the days, now numbered, that she was still spending with her husband. She loved him more than she had ever loved him when he belonged to her, because she could no longer reach him, because already he was mysterious, inaccessible, one of God's elect.

Although they still lived side by side, the distance between them widened. Little by little, the duties of his profession reclaimed him, became all the more absorbing now that he was striving to save souls as well as bodies.

Unostentatiously, yet without deference to the opinions of others, he affirmed his new beliefs whenever the opportunity presented itself. For Maurice Verdon and others of his colleagues, they were the object of hilarity and derision. But not so for the sick. Before performing an operation, he would quietly urge his patient to have confidence, telling him that that morning he had received Communion for him. More often than not, the unbelievers replied prudently and flatteringly that they had perfect confidence in his skill.

Then he would go on, with gentle insistence:

"It is not I. I am only an instrument in the hand of Him who is all-powerful and all-compassionate."

Frequently, upon making a remark of this kind, he saw an expression of astonishment and respect sweep over the face he was watching solicitously, and hope flooded through him.

He tried and succeeded in difficult operations which increased his moral prestige simultaneously with his reputation. The humble faith of the man who was considered one of the greatest surgeons of the day, touched his patients deeply. It became far from rare that those whose physical lives he had saved, asked his guidance in spiritual matters as well. But he could not, personally, see to their conclusion the conversions which he was instrumental in starting. There were times when the penitent whom he had taken to a priest, was unnerved by the first encounter with this unfamiliar personality and, not knowing how to explain himself, and not having the feeling that he was understood, drew back terrified from the heavenly grace. Such defeats produced in Michel a despondency very different in its profundity than that which he experienced when death claimed one of his patients.

"If I had only been a priest," he once said to Adélaide, "that soul would never have been lost."

"You haven't changed a bit from the man you were when you were beginning to practice. You thought you could cure everybody," she said indulgently, pitying his disappointment. "After all, it is not given even to the holiest priest to convert all sinners."

"But he alone possesses the powers which can save, and there are so few to minister to all those who are waiting and suffering in darkness."

Then, heroically, she uttered the words for which he thirsted:

"Be patient, Michel. Some day you will go to those who are calling you and who need you."

More than anyone else, she needed him, but he did not know it. As a man, he was attracted more by the mass than by the individual, more by the general than by the particular. He gave himself wholly, now, to his brothers in Jesus Christ. She felt no resentment, judging that she was not worthy alone to occupy his heart.

She was very lonely. She had been too absorbed in her love to have either the time or the desire to make real friendships. Her brother was unforgiving on the subject of her conversion. Of the numerous acquaintances that she formerly had had, none was intimate enough to come to seek her out in her self-imposed solitude. The new converts whom Michel brought to his home, found her cold and distant and incomprehensible, and secretly held it against her that she did not wear that look of radiant joy which they thought fitting for a Christian. She felt no quickening of her heart now at being with her husband. Nights of intimacy no longer drew them together, and in the daytime they scarcely saw each other. Michel operated very early and in consequence he had to attend first Mass. They lunched late and hastily. His consultations lasted all afternoon, and in the evening weariness soon overcame him. His wife who lived beside him and whom he thought he knew so well, gradually became a stranger to him once more. He did not know that she was suffering, for she did not complain. Her soul which at the command of love had opened to him utterly, was closing now. Forsaken, Adélaide offered her barren heart to God.

They lived on the Boulevard des Invalides. The Benedictine chapel in the Rue Monsieur became for her what the abbey at Evolayne had been, the center of her religious life. Every morning she went there to Mass and returned in the afternoon for vespers. She chose a seat directly in front of the grille; a feeling came over her there that she and the nuns whom she did not know were linked in comradeship and understanding. She listened, much moved, to their ethereal voices and to the intermittent rustling, like a breeze through a forest, as they knelt and rose again. How beautiful it was, this place where the Creator, invisible, offered Himself to the worship of those unseen creatures, who had taken Him as their spouse. She felt a presence manifest there, while outside, the streets swarming with people like automatons driven by an unseen mechanism, seemed empty and lifeless to her.

She forgot her own existence by losing herself in the existence of Him whose life the liturgical year unfolded before her eyes and which, for the first time since her childhood, she followed day by day.

She saw the Almighty, in the helplessness of infancy and poverty, born in a manger. She worshiped Him with the wise men and the shepherds. His marvelous life was lived once more before her, amid the splendor of His miracles and the tenderness of His parables. Across the ages, on the roads of Palestine, she went to meet Him whose words were of light, and truth, and forgiveness alone. She mingled with the sick who came to Him to be healed. She was as one with the apostles who, at the call of the Lamb of God, without yet clearly understanding why, left all things to follow Him. She was among the enthusiastic crowd which acclaimed the Son of David and spread palm branches in His path in that apotheosis of His entry into Jerusalem. The very ceremony which commemorated Christ's victory, threw into greater relief His apparent defeat. The Church showed Him simultaneously in his twofold triumph, that of Palms and that of the Cross, as if to signify that His kingdom was not of this world, and that He wished to regain it only through humiliation, and torture, and death.

The tragedy of Holy Week began. The Son of God drank to the dregs the cup of human suffering, took upon Himself all the sins of the world. Innocent, He gave Himself up to angry justice. The offices became more numerous. In all the churches, the clergy assembled for long ceremonies, to reconstitute and reënact the drama of the Passion. They adopted the words of the prophets to announce and lament the death of the Savior. Down through the centuries, Christ's plaintive cry came unceasingly, shaking the world. To the lamentations of His children, to their sufferings, He answered with His own eternal agony and His pathetic pleading:

O, all ye who pass by the way,
Attend and see
If there be any sorrow!

O, my people,
What more should I have done for thee,
That I have not done?

I have planted thee
As the fairest of my vineyards
And now
You are become unto me
Exceeding bitterness.

But among all His children, filled as were their hearts with love for Him as they went from church to church, visiting the repositories strewn with flowers, and piously kissing the Cross, how few comprehended the full significance of His lament!

Adélaide pictured herself on Calvary at the foot of the Cross, a desolate and faithful Magdalene. The utter abandonment of the Son of God touched her who was also abandoned. She had no answer to Christ's words of reproach. Her unrequited love lifted in passionate sympathy toward His love by faithless men contemned. On Good Friday afternoon, having been unable to receive Holy Communion that day, kneeling in the deserted church before the empty tabernacle, she had an impression that life was being withdrawn from her, felt in an almost physical way the awful privation of God.

"Christ is risen again!"

It was with that exclamation of deliverance that she greeted her husband when she met him as they left the church after the office of Holy Saturday. Michel's eyes, at once glad and grave, rested on her.

"Yes, Adé, and we too have risen again," he said. "Only a little time ago, our souls were dead within us. The Lord has breathed upon them, has drawn them from the tomb. How can we ever show our gratitude for His boundless mercy? The sacrifice of both our lives is scarcely great enough."

"May it be accepted," she said fervently.

Easter week was gray and rainy, but under the wind and wet, the sap began to stir. With the first fine day, the buds on the trees opened. Then the chestnut trees burst into flower. Here and there a few lilacs hung heavy over rare garden walls. Spring came everywhere with a rush. For Adélaide, it was torturing in its beauty. It was life's final call and she could not prevent herself from answering. She began to go out more often, felt once more the desire to be beautiful, took delight in shopping for fine, soft, gay-colored materials. Occasionally, in the evening, she again went to a concert or to the theater. It was spring in her soul also, and her desire for love blossomed for a last time, before it was withered and scattered by the sultry wind of solitude. During those days, there were not enough churches in Paris to shelter her weakness. Even in them, memories of bygone happiness, and youth, and overflowing tenderness obsessed her. Only after hours of prayer and struggle could she recapture the placidity which only an empty heart can know. She remained for long periods at a time between the stern walls which protected her frailty. And comparing the security which she felt there with the uneasiness which overcame her outside, she believed she could no longer endure any life save that of the cloister.

It was she who first asked her husband, toward the beginning of June:

"When do we leave for Evolayne?"

Perhaps without confessing it, she hoped he might give a gesture of surprise and a vague, evasive answer. But Michel had refrained from speaking of their plans only because he thought his wife was wholly in accord with him concerning them.

"I shall be free in July," he said simply. "I have made all arrangements to be relieved for three months again this year. We shall want to stay at the abbey a long time so that Father Athanase will have every opportunity to examine us thoroughly."

She dropped her head in sign of acquiescence. She felt spiritless and beaten and indifferent to everything. Tired by the perpetual effort which it required of her to live side by side with Michel as a stranger, she longed to be only a nameless nun, without personality of her own, forgotten by everyone, hidden in God.

VIII

.PRUDENT as Father Athanase was, he could no longer refuse to listen seriously to the two penitents who, after a year, came back to him with their desires unchanged. Now, the problem of their remarkable, double vocation had, at least, to be examined, even if it could not be resolved. And the monk applied himself to it, not without misgivings, but with all the zeal and circumspection and impartiality which the circumstances required.

As far as Michel was concerned, his mind was soon made up. It was Adélaide who made him uneasy. Yet he had to admit to himself that she seemed transformed, better balanced and more calm than the year before. He found no trace of that exaltation which so often unbalances women's judgment. She spoke little, but what she said was clear and to the point. She declared that worldly happiness was no longer sufficient for her, but at the same time she admitted that she was terrified by the sacrifice which was required of her. That fear pleased the monk, for he would have been wary of too great ardor and certainty.

Nonetheless, he recalled her hysteria, soon after

129

she had been converted, when she feared that her husband was deserting her to enter a cloister. How did it happen that she had been the first to suggest that she follow him? How was it that instead of restraining him, she had released him of all his obligations to her? By what miracle had that jealous, loving wife, who even thought of herself as the rival of God, been turned into this self-effacing woman who voluntarily renounced all worldly joy?

Without daring to answer those questions, Father Athanase felt himself shaken. He no longer spared his penitent. His direction, lenient hitherto, became more strict, even rigorous in its demands on her strength and her determination. He no longer treated her as a woman of the world, a poor, weak being in whom one must look for only a little good will, but as a nun. He set upon all her habits of self-indulgence, regulated her life hour by hour, demanded an absolute, unresisting obedience, and always he found her docile. Her faith seemed firm, her piety unassailable, her heart humble and open. The monk marveled in silence.

Fearing to trust his own unsupported impressions, he wished his friends to be examined by the Father Abbot. The latter received them one day and questioned them for several hours. It was Michel who replied for both. Adélaide limited herself to approving his words, certain that in explaining his soul he was explaining her own. The Father Abbot knew that men are much more rarely called than women, and, in interrogating the two neophytes, he concerned himself primarily with the man. The woman's voluntary effacement allowed him no opportunity to gauge her personality. He saw her only as a gentle, pious creature, the counterpart of her husband. By every standard, Michel was already far advanced in the ways of mysticism, and entirely detached from the world. The abbot thought that in judging the husband he was judging the wife as well.

"Two singularly favored souls, my son," he said to Father Athanase.

Fortified by the opinion of his spiritual superior, the monk then sent his penitent to make a retreat at the monastery of Helmancourt, for the Benedictine Order alone appealed to her as it did Michel. Adélaide was received tenderly by a frail, young, little nun who, despite her stature, had about her an aura of strength and dignity, and whose dark eyes shone with kindliness. Mother Hermengarde, the abbess of the monastery, was warm-hearted and sympathetic. She felt instantly drawn toward this convert whose story moved her profoundly. As soon as she felt that she had won Adélaide's confidence, she asked her to tell her about her life. She marveled at the soul which was opened to her. It seemed evident to her that a woman who had once been so happy, who had loved purely and been loved in return, could not renounce those joys except through a very special grace from God.

When the case had been thoroughly studied in both monasteries, Father Athanase was charged to transmit to his friends a favorable, yet at the same time prudent, opinion.

"Your vocation," he told them, "seems genuine, but you will agree that it must be established beyond a doubt before presenting your request to the authorities. You have undergone a year's test together without your resolution faltering. We think it would be well now to impose on you a first, merely temporary separation, while you are yet of the world. I would suggest that Michel go back to his duties in Paris and you, Madame, might spend the year in another city, any one that you may choose. If that separation doesn't prove intolerable to you, and if, in a year, your determination still persists, then it will be time to present your case to your bishop and petition Rome for the authorization necessary for your simultaneous entrance into the cloister. Think carefully before giving me your answer. You can tell me in a few days whether you are ready to follow this advice, or whether you have any objection to offer."

Together Michel and Adélaide left the visitors' parlor where the priest had received them after vespers. And as the day was scorching and it was still mid-afternoon, they turned their steps toward the wood. Under the leafy roof, the hot, breathless air seemed as oppressive as if they were indoors. They walked very slowly, close to one another. Adélaide felt crushed and heart-sick, utterly lost. She dared not speak to her husband, sure that he would not be sharing her suffering; doubtless these delays that seemed so short to her, were discouragingly long to him. They came to a place where two paths crossed and she asked mechanically:

"Right or left?"

He did not answer and turning her head a little she saw that he was looking at her, not with that distracted indifference which had given her so much pain, but as he had in the days when they had been most deeply in love. He was looking at her eyes, and her mouth, and her hands, and her body. He was looking at her soul, at her tenderness for him. And at the same time he was thinking of that immense treasure of memories which they possessed in common, of all that she offered to him in so many happy hours together. Suddenly he held out his hand to her with a cry:

"My joy, my darling, how can I lose you!"

She flung herself against him, sobbing, and he strained her to him so close that she felt the bones of his face against her own, while their tears mingled and his arms encircled her in an embrace which seemed eternal. She thought it was a revelation of their common weakness and when he drew away, pale, his brow damp, she murmured:

"It's too much, Michel, it's too great a sacrifice."

But he remained strong, even in his emotion never losing sight of his objective.

"Christ also hesitated before quaffing the bitter cup," he said.

He did not consider that the anguish before which a God had shown weakness, might well exceed the strength of a human being. He judged his companion by himself. But the sword which had left only a passing wound in him, lay buried in her heart, threatening the very wellsprings of life.

"I would rather die," she moaned, clinging to him.

He kept one arm about her, and with the other he stroked her hair, comforting her.

"Let us be proud, my darling, that we have been chosen for this absolute gift of ourselves. Above all, we must not resist God's demands, terrible as they seem, but give thanks for our suffering, knowing how necessary it is to us. Don't you feel already how it purifies us even as it wounds us, how sweet it is beneath its cruelty?"

Adélaide warned him, then, when she moaned:

"It is not the same suffering for you, Michel, and for me."

He only half believed her. He knew of course that she was weaker than he, but today her weakness seemed to him a temptation against which he should defend himself as well as his wife.

"Let us not pity each other too much," he said

gently. "The hardest thing for us both is for me to reconcile myself to your suffering, and you to mine."

But she would have welcomed seeing him suffer as she had suffered during all the time when he had been less concerned about losing her than in not being able to leave her. She tried, timidly, to soften him further.

"Is all this really required of us, Michel? I am not so sure any more."

He looked at her in surprise.

"And where could the idea have come to you from, if God had not inspired it? What human motive could ever have impelled you to be the first to suggest such a sacrifice?"

She found nothing to reply. She had suffered cruelly in perceiving that she was no longer Michel's only love. However there was no proof that she might not have won him back if she had made the attempt. Instead of defending her love, she had immediately admitted her defeat. How could she explain the sudden despair which had made her surrender so easily, when nothing was lost? High-strung natures often pass quickly from the heights of ecstasy to the depths of despair. They can exist only in the fullness of joy or grief, abundance or misery; the middle ground is intolerable to them. Thus when their happiness totters, one often sees them take a savage delight in destroying it completely. But Adélaide, though she realized that she had gone to an extreme, did not understand the reason why.

"Don't you feel," Michel went on, "how ephemeral are the things of the earth? Was our love truly sufficient for you? Were you perfectly content?"

Perfectly! That word was so inappropriate for a human happiness that was prey to a thousand accidents, to old age, to death. She shook her head with a smile that verged on tears. Michel took her hand.

"God alone is everything for you, as He is for me."

She could not feel convinced. Except for the moments when exaltation dominated her and made everything easy, she was only an indecisive woman, incapable of resolutely making up her mind. Now that she had to make so momentous a choice, one on which her whole life depended, the terrors of uncertainty beset her. Within the space of a few hours she veered completely from one determination to another, advancing, retreating, embracing God, then the world, until at last she was like an exhausted beast, lying bleeding on the ground, unable to make another move.

Michel saw her anguish, but he did not help her to overcome it. At any other time, he would have advised her and inspirited her and comforted her, assuming the greater part of the responsibility. But in the present instance, his duty was to remain neutral. He thought at first that she would conquer her weakness quickly, but as time went on and he saw her daily more at sea, he began to suffer. She had betrayed him cruelly, having lured him on by a hope which could not be realized.

With his every thought and desire dedicated to God, he could scarcely tolerate this love which he inspired and which was his chain. When she looked at him fixedly, her eyes full of tears at the realization that she would lose him soon, he would turn away impatiently, then, touched by her hurt, and reproaching himself for his callousness, he would come back and try to console her.

But the friendship which had bound them together seemed dead. They could no longer explain their feelings to each other. Adélaide dared not confess to her husband how much she loved him, nor he, how much he longed to leave her. And when they questioned each other, in an effort to break down the barriers, their replies were ambiguous, for the truth would have wounded them too much.

"Michel," asked Adélaide, "is the idea of living in the world intolerable to you now? Tell me frankly, could you bear it?"

"I am ready to take it up with you again tomorrow, if the cloister has ceased to attract you."

"I didn't say that," she protested. "I don't know yet. I must think."

One day, however, she broke down in a confession of her misery and her fear.

"After all, why do we aim so high? Isn't it enough

to remain in the way of life in which God placed us? Marriage, imperfect as it is, is not sinful. One can achieve salvation in it."

"Without any doubt," he agreed. "True, it would have been beautiful to have renounced everything for God, to have offered Him a happiness of which we were not weary. Those were your words one day, and I admired you for them. Does it seem too great a sacrifice to you now? Well, it's very beautiful even to have aspired to it. Let's not think about it any more, my poor child."

She could not endure that condescending tone, at the same time so gentle and so scornful. She was tortured by the idea of betraying the confidence which he had put in tune, bent on the same ideal?

The struggle went on and on without coming to solution. For months she was a hunted thing. She was unhappy when she was with Michel, but as soon as he went away she felt the unendurable deprivation of his absence. It no longer brought her comfort to go into the woods and fields. At the abbey, her prayer was one long agony and when, by chance, a moment of peace came to her, she took fright, fearing that she might not be able to escape from some overwhelming grace. During these days, she found no succor save in Father Athanase, who was a firm friend in her time of need. He had foreseen the struggle which she was having, and its long duration only surprised him without disquieting him. At so critical a time, the priest took care not to intervene between her soul and God. But without bringing the least pressure to bear on his penitent, he was of enormous passive help to her. Almost daily, without any sign of weariness, he listened to her lament and sob and take a thousand contrary resolutions, and although women's tears and vacillations were intolerable to him, he remained patient and gentle. The smiling serenity which he brought to her twistings and turnings never failed to reassure her and reduce her grief to more normal proportions. She spoke to him of her inordinate love for Michel.

"It is both natural and permissible that you should love your husband," he said heartily. "You have every right to weep at the thought of leaving him. I would not wish it otherwise."

And when she confessed her fear, he said:

"What nun or priest hasn't known that fear? Why, even the bravest trembles in the face of God's demands upon him."

Finally, one day, paternally and unemotionally, he summed up the situation.

"My dear child, why do you allow yourself to become so wrought up, after all? You say that you feel yourself drawn to the cloister, and you have asked us to examine your vocation. It seems genuine to us but it is too exceptional for us to proceed without the greatest prudence. We are suggesting a new test to you, which in no way commits you for the future and whose sole purpose is to enable you to understand your own heart better. By acting upon that suggestion, you are doing nothing irrevocable. Why tremble and torment yourself in advance? If, in a year, you have changed your mind, you can take up your old life again without the least difficulty."

But Adélaide realized that after a year of separation, Michel, who already had so little in common with her, would come back to her only out of duty, and if she absolutely demanded it. By consenting to leave him, she would be doing something which could never be undone.

"Besides," the monk went on indulgently, seeing her trouble, "the advice that we give you is not an order. You are at liberty not to follow it. I repeat, you are free and no one is trying to force you. Is it Michel that you are concerned about? I will answer for him that he will go back to Paris with you tomorrow if you wish it, and without reproaching you in the slightest. Things are far simpler than you think. All you have to say is, 'I do not wish,' and there will be no further question of what has happened here."

She sat silent, deep in thought. Up until the present, she had trembled to see herself being driven toward the cloister, and now that she was being turned back toward the world, she felt a fear that was greater still. She knew that her life, torn by the spiritual battle that had raged within it, could never again be as it had been. Henceforth she could know only a relative, partial happiness, shallow indeed after the fullness of her anguish. For one who has once heard the call of heroism, all other human aspirations seem insipid. He who has climbed the first peaks of sacrifice turns back with difficulty. From the heights where she had ventured, Adélaide looked down at her past and found it uninviting.

"It is strange, Father, but I have no desire to go back to Paris, to take up my old life. . . ."

She saw the monk smile, and smiled in turn with a feeling of release. She thought that now she understood herself, and a sensation of peace flooded through her.

She determined to make another retreat at Helmancourt, and she spent an entire week there, sharing the life of the nuns and living in accordance with monastic discipline. Within those walls redolent of prayer, meditation seemed a natural state. Her disquietude vanished almost like a puff of smoke in the salutary, tranquil atmosphere of the convent where so many fervent souls were secretly interceding for her. Her life, her feverish life, was as if suspended. No more balancing of this with that, no more alternatives, no more struggle—only grateful surcease for her weary heart. The cloister about her reassured her. Michel's absence, far from seeming cruel to her, allowed her a deeper peace. Mother Hermengarde's affection was doubly sweet to her who had never had a friend of her own sex.

"I have been very happy here, Mother," she said to the abbess the day before her departure. "I have been at peace."

"I think," the nun answered, "you will be coming back to us, to stay."

Once more, Adélaide explained her doubts concerning her vocation. But to Mother Hermengarde, human love was a manifestation of the divine.

"It has its source in God," she said. "Why should it not lead back to him? You know, my child, that only in heaven do the imperfect unions of the earth reach their full flowering and perfection. If we consider things in the light of the eternal, what is this brief life? What is the sacrifice of an instant? That which is asked of you today astonishes you because your happiness was not sinful. Who knows? Perhaps, in loving one human being so ardently, you were running the risk of preferring him to the Creator; and so, perhaps, you have been chosen to make amends, by your noble example, for the divorce and the adultery which are the abomination of our time. In any event, you have nothing to lose. Come, make a gift of your happiness, because, as I say, it is the question only of an instant. Separated from your husband, you will feel him closer to you. God is taking him only to give him back to you when you will have learned, at the foot of His altars, what true love is."

Her fervent, lofty words lifted Adélaide above the

142

earth. One day more she prayed, with her soul tense in an effort that was both thoughtless of herself and easy.

She left Helmancourt after vespers and turned toward Evolayne. The road running along the hill was bordered by clumps of fir: lordly, straight trees, unmoving in the breeze, through which the light filtered dimly. In their shade, the tranquillity of the cloister persisted. Adélaide felt no qualms as she saw Michel coming to meet her. He was walking slowly, seemingly hesitant, for he was expecting a definite answer which could crown or shatter his life, and she knew he feared the words she was going to say.

"Good evening, Michel, my brother," she said, pressing his hand.

Startled at the name she gave him, he threw a quick glance at her, hope trembling in his eyes. Still he said nothing, fearing he might have misunderstood. She hastened to reassure him:

"I am willing to accept the test that is imposed on us; I accept from now on whatever God may wish to require of us."

Without any selfish reservations, she relished the joy which she had just given him. For she could endure now the sweet, thrilling pain of the sword which she carried in her heart unceasingly because of him; her patient love could wait until eternity. She smiled, her soul as tranquil as the shadowy woods where, that evening, they were exchanging their first farewell.

"I renounce you, Michel," she said simply.

"I renounce you," he repeated.

With the words, she had a sensation of deliverance. This human happiness for which she had feared so long, this precarious, unstable, constantly threatened happiness which she had had to defend so fiercely and unremittingly, finally slipped and crashed, broken by circumstances and by her own will. Freed from that burden, she had nothing more that could be taken from her.

PART TWO

I. "NO doubt you have revealed everything that you have just told me to your confessor?"

Mother Hermengarde had put the question negligently, pushing her chair over between the two long windows of her small oratory so that the light came from behind her back. The pale winter sun spared the indecision on her countenance and fell on the nun who was sitting on a low chair opposite her.

Thus placed, the abbess was able more easily to scrutinize the face of Adélaide, in religion Mother Constance. It bore little resemblance to the ordinary nun's face. Theirs are for the most part meek and passive, and even when their downcast eyes are lifted up, they are like spotless panes of glass reflecting nothing. After seven years in the cloister, Adélaide's features, notwithstanding her wimple and veil, were vibrant with expression. No discipline of will could prevent them betraying the slightest of her emotions. At the moment, they showed a quick consternation.

"I don't believe . . . no, I don't think . . . It's so difficult . . . however, I had no intention of hiding anything from Father Gontran. . . ."

147

"I am sure of it, my child," said the abbess, allaying with a gesture the dismay she had awakened.

The reply, as a matter of fact, did not surprise her. The soul which she had just been examining in the course of a long interview was guilty of no fault grave enough or singular enough to arrest the attention of a confessor. It required all the knowledge that a superior has of her daughters to discern the seriousness of the evil which lay hidden in the mind of this one. The constant weariness, the lack of any perceptible inclination toward prayer or communion, of which Adélaide had complained, her longing for the past, the smothered importunities of her heart and flesh, her acceptance of suffering but her failure to dominate it, her doubts, all these held nothing particularly disturbing in themselves. Many of the religious had gone through similar crises and had emerged stronger after their weakness. And they had used the same words to describe their spiritual dilemma as their sister, more gravely stricken, had just used; for no language is rich enough to express the thousand nuances of feeling and temptation which might at first glance seem similar. But the abbess, supplementing through intuition the inadequacy of the replies, listened primarily to the hidden voices which accompanied and completed them. Experienced as she was, and sure in her judgments, she was hesitant before so exceptional a problem.

She was astonished that it had taken her this long

to understand one of her daughters, the very one, indeed, over whom she had watched with the greatest solicitude. As a novice, she had given every hope; her selflessness had been such that nothing counted beside it. Mother Hermengarde had even dreamed of saintliness for her. For a long time, Adélaide had been wholly docile in her hands, submissive to her firm, wise direction. Then the abbess had begun to notice a slight but sustained resistance, an involuntary withdrawal. In her efforts to win Adélaide's confidence more fully she had encountered a frightened being who shrank into silence. And now that the crisis, which she had feared had come, it proved even more serious than she had anticipated, taking on the proportions of a disaster. The soul which had seemed so beautiful was revealed as devoid of will-power, without true virtue, without other strength than exaltation. Her piety was all emotion; it had no solidity. The splendor of her intentions had no basis in character. At the first puff of wind, the whole fragile edifice had crumbled in ruins. Probing that troubled mind, the abbess had been unable to find peace anywhere. Beneath the anguish, and the uncertainty, and the discouragement, she had found only emptiness. There was not a single stronghold of the spirit where reason might immure itself and give battle.

The evil had been creeping, hidden and insidious, for a long time. And she, the very fiber of whose being it was undermining, was discovering it only

149

too late. At that very moment, Adélaide, thinking back over her past, was similarly astonished to see such contrast in it: a sure, continuous, unwavering ascent, followed by a dizzy fall. Not once, during the period of trial which had been imposed on her in the world, away from Michel, nor during the five years which preceded her final vows, had she called into question the genuineness of her vocation. Behind her, there was only an abyss of grief and a shattered life which she could not think of resuming. She had gone ahead bravely toward those pure, barren regions where her husband wished to live.

She had seemed destined to make a good nun. The time of her postulancy had passed easily and without rebellion. Fatigue had been her greatest aid at first. Passing from the soft, easy life of the world to the carefully regulated, though not excessively austere, existence of the Benedictines, she had been, so to speak, freed from her own personality. For months, she was so worn out by physical exertion that she could scarcely think at all. Then when her body had been hardened to the discipline of monastic life, her soul was already habituated to the atmosphere of the cloister. She felt a part of it. The strangeness and confusion of the first weeks gave way to a wave of enthusiasm and an appetite for sacrifice at which she was amazed. The rule which usually was hardest to accept, that of obedience, seemed relatively easy to her. She loved Mother Hermengarde, for she was intelligent and understanding and commanding of respect, albeit firm and severe when necessity demanded. Moreover, from a distance, Michel was an immense source of strength. By common agreement, the two communities had decided to grant special consideration to them because of their separation. Until they had pronounced their final vows, it was decided that they might write each other once a month, except during the penitential seasons of Lent and Advent. Those letters nurtured Adélaïde's spiritual life, periodically gave it fresh impetus. Involuntarily, in her replies, she imitated their mystic tone, and always quick to think herself of the same mind as he whom she loved, she filled them with expressions of heavenly aspiration and scorn for the joys of the world.

Two years before, on the same day as he, she had taken her final vows. As she had committed her life forever, her heart had been serene and filled with confidence. Nevertheless, when she analyzed it carefully, she realized that it was on that day that her spiritual progress had ceased. Almost immediately afterward she was stricken with pleurisy, and in the prostration following her illness, then in the weakness and idleness of her convalescence, she lost the tranquillity which she had so laboriously built up. Cured, but weakened in spirit even more than in body, she had found herself on earth once more, her wings broken, harassed by doubts, thirsting for happiness, overwhelmed by problems which for so long a time she had refused to admit to herself or to anyone else. After all the years which she had spent purging her heart of human images, she saw them reappearing everywhere on the walls of her memory. Since Michel had ceased to write to her, he had no longer been a guide supporting her and preceding her along the road of sacrifice, but a silent tempter dragging her back. Knowing that the future would not restore him to her, she sought him in the past. And the thought came to her that it had been only the feeling of temporariness which had allowed her to be happy in the convent, since as soon as her life was pledged she had felt a horror for the grilles which were shut upon her forever. Suddenly she thought she understood the problem which she was really examining today for the first time and the truth was so frightful that it burst from her in a cry:

"O, Mother, what have I done? I have made a mistake, I have been deceived, it is another's will which brought me here."

It was as if the abbess had heard her own thoughts put into words, and had she been less mistress of herself she might have betrayed her consternation by a look or a gesture or too hasty a protest. But she was on her guard, for she knew that the greatest danger threatening Adélaide was despair. She smiled her luminous, reassuring smile and, as if she thought the nun's words of little consequence, did not reply to them directly.

"The cloister is not an easy place," she said poisedly. "One must expect to suffer in it. You must not hope to be always uplifted by grace. When that grace is withdrawn from you, you have no right to doubt your vocation. In these moments of despondency you should be calm. There isn't a nun who hasn't experienced this aridity, these doubts of which you are complaining."

"Temporarily perhaps, but I have been suffering from them for nearly two years."

"Two years! Ever since your pleurisy, you mean?" exclaimed the other with a note of relief in her voice. She had just found an explanation which she herself might believe.

"You think your soul is wavering because your body is weak, because your whole system is still shaken. You are misinterpreting and exaggerating a trouble which has purely a physical cause."

Adélaide did not appear convinced.

"Are you sure? Isn't it rather that my illness has revealed me to myself? O, Mother, what shall I do?"

Her cry, like a hurt child's, brought the Mother Superior to a sudden decision. Her face became radiant with kindness and comfort. She laid her two hands on Mother Constance's shoulders, forcing herself to instill in her a confidence which she did not have.

"Sleep," she said with authority.

And, as the nun looked up questioningly in surprise, she explained:

"Yes, my child, sleep. That is all I require of you. You are worn out with anxiety. Even your prayer is bad because it is entangled with problems which it cannot solve. You must rest. I shall shorten your hours of prayer and the period of seclusion in your cell. Let your sisters and myself pray in your place. Don't be afraid, don't question the future any more. Trust in us."

During the weeks which followed, the abbess's direction was a masterpiece of prudence and tenderness. Her entire attention was concentrated on Mother Constance. She excused her from long offices, gave her more strengthening food, assigned her tasks outdoors which were not too tiring but which allowed her no opportunity for reverie. At the same time that she was thus taking action practically, she was taking action spiritually. By her order, the whole community drew about the soul in peril, shielded it with bucklers of prayer. Adélaide tried obediently not to think any more; she let herself be borne along, so to speak, by the solicitude which surrounded her. But she remained incapable of disciplining her thoughts. The cloister no longer defended her against the intrusion of worldly desires, it shut in only her body. She continued to say the prayers, to go through the motions of a nun, but every unguarded thought turned to her former life. She was always at Michel's side, alone with him, given wholly to him.

The moment was approaching when he was to be ordained priest. For the last time he received permission to write to his wife, to inform her that the ceremony had been fixed for the following month.

"I am waiting in peace," he wrote, "for that glorious day, the day which crowns our life. I shall not kneel alone at the foot of the altar; you will be at my side. My sacrifice is, above all, yours. You have done more than permit it, you were the first to wish it. . . ."

After taking cognizance of the letter, the abbess handed it to Adélaide. The latter read it several times with growing emotion. She cried for a long time, whether from grief or joy she could not tell.

"Be glad, my child," Mother Hermengarde exhorted her; "we other nuns have only our own lives to offer. You are more favored, richer than we. In giving yourself, you are giving a priest to God."

"Yes," murmured Adélaide. "I am very proud."

For a moment she felt strong, inspired by the weight of her cross, then, almost immediately, her heart broke under her too heavy burden, cried out in its anguish.

"O, but Mother, wouldn't I have done better to keep him? He could have lived more easily away from the altar than I away from him. I wanted him to be happy, but his happiness isn't enough for me.

All I needed was for him to be near me. Even that year when I was living beside him and was nothing to him, that barren year when I suffered so much, seems like paradise. You said to me that 'separated from your husband, you will feel him close to you.' What is this mystic union that is so pure and so cold? . . . Here I am a nun and he a priest, and God sees us, blesses us, loves us, will bring us together again, but that doesn't give me happiness; it's either not enough or too much. I am cold and all I know is that I want him beside me, his hand in mine, his heart near mine. . . ."

The abbess let her go on sobbing out her grief for a long time without interrupting her. She was convinced now that in immolating herself in the cloister, Adélaide had obeyed only the dictates of an heroic exaltation. The certainty saddened her without shaking her confidence, for she knew how mysterious are the designs of God and how unexpected His means of executing them. There was still one hope. The love which was harmful now might become beneficial if the spiritual side of it alone could be retained. This became Mother Hermengarde's aim. But the guidance which she tried to give had to be as adroit as it was delicate. She was careful not to use constraint or authority. Putting aside her rôle as Superior, she acted with Adélaide as a wise younger woman might have acted who was trying to help a friend unhappy in love. Almost daily, she called Adélaide into her own oratory and talked to her very simply about Michel. It was of the greatest importance that she should not lose herself in a passion which was now unrealizable, that she should not allow herself to feed upon it with an ever-growing sense of guilt. She must not feel that she was sinful or accursed because she was in love. Gently, the abbess reasoned with her and reassured her.

"You have a perfect right to grieve for your husband, and it is only natural that at this particular time your separation should seem more than ordinarily hard to you. However good a Christian she may be, a mother whose son is about to be ordained priest cannot keep herself from crying. Yet she has known all along that her son would leave her some day. How much more difficult it is for a wife, who has believed that her husband would belong to her always. Such a bond cannot be broken without the heart bleeding, and it is nothing to be wondered at. My dear child, it is permissible to love in the cloister. All that is necessary is that God be first. Have courage. These are the last struggles of the woman within you."

Adélaide was comforted by these talks. Then, again, she would fall into deep despondency. Never losing heart, the abbess roused her, strengthened her, counseled her tenderly and at last put her to a test which might prove decisive. Ten days before Michel's ordination, she bade her to prepare herself for it by a novena, and added:

"I have requested that your husband should say his first Mass in our monastery. You will be allowed to speak to him afterwards for a moment."

For those endowed with vivid imagination, a moment in time can exert an extraordinary fascination. When circumstances conspire to make a single hour loom above the dim, colorless round of future days, that crowning hour can eclipse, for them, all that have preceded and all that are to follow it, can render them oblivious to everything else. To be able to live it justifies any suffering in their eyes.

The dispensation accorded the husband and wife was not without precedent. Adélaide had known for a long time that she would be permitted to see Michel as a priest; that one day, one single time, she would receive Communion from his hand. That hope had shone like a far-off light on the bleak, imprisoning horizon of her life, and now it was very close. Essentially emotional, she had always sought emotion as a happiness in itself. The one now promised her filled to overflowing the cup which had been empty. She was as if hypnotized by the joy to come. The future did not extend beyond the one blessed moment which she prolonged into eternity. Her fears, her torments, her doubts fell away from her. No other feeling remained in her save that of waiting.

Watching over her ceaselessly, the abbess was astonished by the calm which that spell induced in her. She redoubled her prayers that heaven might bestow its benediction upon that last reunion of husband and wife. Obsessed as Adélaide was by a phantom, in love with a man who no longer existed save in her memory, she might find poise once more in seeing him before her in all his inaccessibility as a priest. God might make use of this man, who was too much beloved, to strengthen the troubled but courageous soul that was striving so sincerely, whose very passion remained so noble, and who was so well deserving of His grace and peace.

II. THE day Michel was ordained passed for Adélaide in a sort of ecstasy in which her own life was as nothing. Her soul was far away, a witness of the ceremony which was taking place in Evolayne. She followed every detail, experienced every emotion. She was never absent from her husband's side and feeling already the influence of his presence, she persuaded herself that the next day he would be able to dispel all her doubts and give her peace.

The hour came at last when kneeling in her customary place in the stalls she saw her beloved, clad in the priestly garments, advancing toward the altar. The Mass was celebrated with especial pomp that morning. Father Athanase assisted his friend who was performing the sacred rites for the first time. Through the grille which divided the nave in two, separating the nuns from the choir, through the tears which dimmed her eyes, Adélaide could see her husband only indistinctly. She had the impression of being in the midst of a storm. Occasionally, as if in a flash of lightning, she caught a clear glimpse of Michel's tall figure, his tonsured head, his face as he turned toward the congregation, his uplifted arms. Then night closed in about her once more, while the cherished voice still reached her, soft and resonant, breaking a little at the end of the Latin phrases. She could not sing the office with her sisters. The abbess, foreseeing the emotion she would experience, had excused her from it. Silently, in spirit, she united herself with the man of God who, to her, was at the same time the sacrificer and the sacrificed. She prayed as she had never prayed before:

"Make me worthy of him, let me give myself entirely as he has given himself."

Slowly her soul took on a warmth the source of which she could not trace, but which gave her assurance. So rare an hour could not be unavailing. Her doubts would vanish. She waited confidently for God's answer, for the light.

The moment for Communion had come. One by one the nuns advanced to the grille, knelt before the narrow opening behind which Michel awaited them, pyx in hand. In her turn, Adélaide knelt before her husband. Perhaps he did not recognize that dark shadow among the other dark shadows whose mouths alone were exposed beneath their veils. He showed no emotion. His voice did not tremble as he repeated the holy words: "Corpus Domini Jesus Christi . . ." But she could not withstand the temptation. Raising her head, she gazed fixedly through her veil at the forgotten face whose expression at that moment was so gentle and calm. Already she was receiving the

Host and the consecrated hand brushed lightly against her lips. Her eyes closed, capturing the living image. Never in her most fervent Communions had she felt such profound emotion. The human agent suddenly brought fulfillment to that soul which the presence of God left unsatisfied. Certainty, absolute and unquestionable, came to her at last.

"It is he that I loved! I have known no other God." The blinding revelation was followed by a sort of heavy, hateful peace. She had asked for light and she had received it: a chilling, heart-rending light. She made no attempt to struggle against the evidence. On her knees among her companions, her hands joined in the attitude of prayer, she considered in silence the irreparable disaster of her life.

Someone touched her on the shoulder. Mass was over, as were the last chants and thanksgiving. Mechanically, she filed from the chapel with the other nuns. Mother Hermengarde spoke to her:

"Hurry, my child. Father Stéphane is waiting for you in the visiting room."

Father Stéphane! That was the name Michel would carry henceforth until death, that made him a stranger, over whom she had no rights. Their interview was wholly useless now. As long as she had been in doubt, she had persuaded herself that her husband might still convince her by explaining to her a truth which she so imperfectly understood. But now she knew her trouble could not be cured, and that he could give her no aid. It remained only that he should know his error. She had a last confession to make to him. What did it matter whether he condemned her or blamed himself? Henceforth they would both suffer through one another, endlessly.

With a nun's light steps, she moved through the long, stone-flagged corridors, without haste, without apprehension, in a sort of indifferent stupor. But when she entered the enormous visiting room, with the gray light falling from the high windows, a sudden pang shot through her. She crossed hurriedly to the grille which divided the room, and leaned all her weight against it, as if she thought she might break down the barrier. Michel was already there, on the other side. Their eyes met for a moment and the cry which she was about to utter was halted on her lips, for she perceived that he was not looking at her as a woman, but as a nun, the elect of God. He spoke and said:

"My dear sister! . . . And there are other names I might use," he went on. "Aren't you in a certain sense my mother also, since it was you who gave me to God, to the Light? And my daughter, because when a man becomes a priest, along with the responsibility he assumes for souls in general, there are certain ones that are peculiarly his. Your soul, the first that was entrusted to me, will always be dearer to me than any other."

He spoke with a studied unctuousness very different from his old, high-strung reserve. The years in the cloister had re-cast his character; he seemed more free, yet at the same time more restrained. Soft, passionless words came easily to his lips now.

They had seated themselves, one on either side of the grille. Motionless, his hands clasped, his eyes lowered, Michel felt no temptation to look at the woman who was no longer his. Even in this moment he accorded her only a prudent, wholly spiritual, attention. He made himself blind so that she should be only a voice to him. But she did not imitate his circumspection. Having nothing now to struggle against, she allowed her love to swell unchecked. She feasted her eyes upon him, poisoning herself with the image of his face. It was a different face, relaxed, serene. The all-consuming joy within him was reflected in an extraordinary radiance; it seemed to glow behind the lowered lids and the tranquil, unsmiling lips. Adélaide looked upon such peace with sad, timid wonder. Better than anyone else, in the depths of her anguish, she knew the pricelessness of joy. It is something marvelous and soft, as sacred as innocence and the weakness of a child. She could not tear it away from that man whom she loved. It is easy to wound those who are unhappy, but not those who are wrapped in the fragile splendor of an unearthly felicity. Adélaide wished, now, to bear the whole weight of the cross alone, without Michel's knowing.

164

"Tell me you are happy," she said imploringly.

"I lay my happiness at your feet. It is you who are responsible for it. What a destiny mine is, how enviable!"

She stammered:

"You are a priest forever. . . ."

On the monk's face the look of peace deepened.

"Yes, the ceremony is over. I have experienced it all: the charge of the Bishop, the call of the Church, the laying on of hands, that sublime response: 'Now I shall no longer call you my servants but my friends. . . .' And I pictured to myself that day long ago when you and I watched a similar ceremony. How far we have advanced since then, how many graces we have received! There is but one flaw in my happiness: the fear of not being worthy. Will the burden of the priesthood exceed my strength? But when I tremble beneath the weight of it, I think of you. I remember that I am not alone. Beside the priest's life, the life of action, there must be a life of effacement, of meditation, of prayer supporting it. Yours will be that for me. You will aid me constantly, won't you? What is the use of my telling you how much I count upon you? I know that your heart will remain united with mine, as it was before, forever."

She was moved by the beauty of his concept, yet she had no notion that it might be realized. This time she would not let herself be deceived. She had only one thought in her heart: he was going to leave her and for the last time in life she was looking upon his face. The marvelous, long-sought-for, short-lived instant was passing, passing. Each second was born, gave forth its poignant sweetness and sped on without her being able to hold it back. The warmth that came to her from his beloved presence, the light turned upon her by his dear face, would soon be taken from her. Time, as it fled, surfeited her and robbed her simultaneously. The gulf of the future yawned; relentlessly she was being impelled toward it and away from him forever.

However, warned by Mother Hermengarde of his wife's travail of soul, Michel was concerned to help her, to do for her everything that was hoped of him.

"You are not telling me about your own life," he said solicitously. "I am told that you have just gone through a long, painful period."

"Yes . . ." she stammered, "very long . . . for almost two years . . . I have been adrift, unable to find the light."

She heard him sigh behind the grille and when he went on, his voice was filled with sympathy.

"I have prayed often that you might be spared that, that if one of us had to suffer, I might be the one chosen."

She asked eagerly:

"Then you have suffered too?"

"We are in the cloister to suffer," he replied evenly, for the pain of the separation had not been such agony for him that he could not speak of it composedly—"Suffering is our companion throughout our lives. It is God's great gift, the sign of His covenant with us. Sometimes, when the flesh is weak, we fear it, but then all we have to do is consider it with love and humility and immediately it becomes as something blessed. I, too, have had hours of despondency and anguish, but I have never let myself be troubled. I was certain, when my spirit was in the depths of misery, that an all-powerful hand would soon be held out to me, and it was always so. Would that I could transmit my certainty to you. Be courageous, tranquil, do not doubt either God or yourself. It is truly a miracle which brought you into the way which you are now following and no temptation can triumph over you if you do not lose sight of the grace which you have received."

He spoke with a confidence that was absolute. He was a man blinded by happiness, and from the heights to which he had risen he saw the world only in the light of the peace that was within himself. He no longer knew the woman whom he had loved. He wished, and he believed, her to be the same as himself. She sensed that it would be easy to confirm him in his error. She had but one more sacrifice to make: not to let him know that she was suffering through him. All she had to do was be silent, or give him vague, ambiguous answers whose meaning he himself would misconstrue.

"It is true that I doubted my vocation," she said in a strangled voice, "but just now, when I received Communion from your hand, light came to me. I am certain beyond a doubt."

She was not lying and because he failed to look at her face, he did not understand that the certainty was that she had not found the right way.

"God is good," he murmured thankfully. "He has deigned to bless our meeting."

"Our last meeting," she repeated, her words firm and dead. What did it matter to her now whether Michel was beside her or in another world? The grille and that priestly garb which was like an armor over his heart, separated them forever. Michel mistook her meaning.

"I understand," he said. "For one who has found God, no human contact is necessary. Certainly our superiors are so good that under grave circumstances they would grant us permission to see one another, but we shall not ask that favor, shall we, even on the threshold of death? Henceforth, we shall renounce each other entirely. I shall help you by my prayers from afar, and you will help me. I give you rendezvous beyond the earth where we shall no longer be separated."

He raised his head. Slowly his lids lifted and through the grille his eyes fixed themselves on Adélaide. He was according a supreme concession to their love. He wished and permitted that look which is a more intimate exchange between two people than any words can be. He sought those dark pupils which, he thought, would reflect only the peace and glory of God. He wished to see his sister's joy. But she, sensing his purpose and quicker than he, had already veiled her face, pale from the anguish of their separation. He was touched by that gesture, whose significance he did not guess; he admired the self-denial which was unwilling to participate in a last expression of human tenderness.

"So holy," he murmured, "so far surpassing me."

She did not move, she said nothing, refusing herself every palliation. Once more, this time without any illusion, knowing exactly what the sacrifice was costing her, she was giving her beloved to God, free of all chains, of all suspicion, of all remorse. Now her heart cried out to have the precious moment come to an end. Brief as it had been, the pain it had brought was too rending for her to bear it longer. To be alone would be a deliverance.

"Have you nothing more to say to me?" asked Michel.

With an effort, she murmured:

"Go, and be happy."

"At least," he said, "I wish to give you my blessing."

She knelt, accepting the little that he gave. Michel, standing, made a great sign of the cross above her. Then he went away quickly, for the memory of the past was in him also and it was hard for him to leave her. Rising to her feet, clutching the grille, she saw him disappear, saw the door close behind him. Then she turned, ran a few steps and stopped, terrified by the tempest unleashed about her. It was not only her flesh and her heart that were in tumult. The ground under her feet, the arches over her head, a thousand voices in space were crying: "Farewell! Farewell!" It was as if the walls were toppling, the whole world were crumbling. She staggered to right and to left and fell prostrate on the stones.

It was there that Mother Hermengarde found her a quarter of an hour later.

Before leaving Helmancourt, Father Stéphane had given the abbess an entirely mistaken impression of his interview with Adélaide. In his eyes, his wife was happier, more detached, holier than he. The Superior had let herself be persuaded by his words and believed that the long-awaited miracle had finally been accomplished. Consequently the fact that Mother Constance had fainted worried her without revealing to her the true state of affairs. The flesh might weaken while the soul remained strong.

When Adélaide was brought back to consciousness, she attempted no explanation. For days she lay inert, weak as one who has lost a quantity of blood. She did not complain, did not speak, did not seem to hear what was said to her. She refused all nourishment, slept much of the time, and as soon as she was awakened, cried effortlessly and unceasingly. At length, little by little, she began to eat and to try to get up. But fits of coughing kept her weak, and every evening her temperature rose. The pulmonary lesion left by her pleurisy had reopened and the doctor who examined her advised the greatest care. Far from being frightened by his diagnosis, Adélaide seemed to take a certain comfort from it, and as soon as she found herself alone in the infirmary with the abbess, she said:

"It is all for the best this way, Mother; now I shall be able to leave."

The abbess was startled:

"Leave!"

Adélaide looked at her, astonished that the decision so firmly fixed in her own mind was not known to others as well.

"Haven't I told you?" she asked. "That's true, I have slept so long! I must have dreamed that I was talking to you. . . . Mother, I cannot remain in the cloister. What I had to do here is done. Michel is a priest, freed from me, given wholly to God. He has no more need of my being imprisoned behind a grille."

There was no bitterness in her voice. Through force of suffering she had become almost insensible.

"Everything makes it easy," she went on. "My state of health gives me a motive for asking to be relieved of my vows. I shall be able to leave without any reproaches. You will not try to keep me here."

She spoke with a gentle firmness that was impressive. It seemed as if she had already shaken off all the ties of the religious life. She no longer addressed the abbess as a respected superior whose advice is accepted submissively, but as a friend, as an equal, bound to her in secret conspiracy. Everything was absolutely clear to her now. She no longer believed in her vocation, and she knew the abbess did not believe in it any more than she. She revealed their strange understanding in those last words: "You will not try to keep me here." And, indeed, Mother Hermengarde did not dare. Appalling as was this disaster, she saw no means of remedying it.

"Where will you go?"

Adélaide made a vague gesture.

"The world is large enough to swallow me."

The abbess went on almost imploringly.

"Reflect well upon it, my child. Your life will be miserable."

"Yes, I know. But to remain here because Michel has cast me off, because I have nothing better to do—Mother, you would not ask it of me. It would be worthy neither of you nor of me."

Once more Mother Hermengarde felt herself dominated. She had too much respect for this misguided but sincere soul to urge the cowardly acceptance of a monastic existence which was not made beautiful by the love of God, which habit alone would render bearable. Nevertheless, the dangers which lay in wait in the world for a woman whose human happiness had been so cruelly dealt with, could not fail to fill her with foreboding. She made a last effort.

"No one can hold you against your wish," she said sadly, "but I urge you to consider it still further. Have you thought that we would of course have to tell Father Stéphane of your departure, and that he would ask the reasons for it and that you would risk destroying his happiness and his peace?"

"Mother, I am no longer equal to it. You must tell him that I am sick, that I am physically incapable of enduring the discipline of the Order. He won't ask any more. He won't look back into the past, he won't guess that in taking the veil I sacrificed myself for him. He will forget me quickly. And I want to forget him. I never shall, here in this atmosphere where everything is redolent of his nearness, where everything about me reminds me of what I have suffered for him. I want to rid myself of the spell of all this. I need to be alone to examine myself, to be free to seek a new life. I don't know what the future holds for me, what I am going to do. But I do know one thing: that is that my place is not in the cloister and that I will not remain in it without vocation."

She looked at Mother Hermengarde and suddenly held out her arms to her in a graceful, impulsive gesture of affection.

"You are the only one I shall miss, Mother. You are the only one who has loved me! . . ."

Loved her too much! To her distress, the abbess realized how dearly among all her daughters, she had cherished this one. And because she reproached herself for being guilty of such forbidden partiality, she appeared not to notice the gesture, steeled herself against the appeal in the lovely, tearful face. Silently, feeling that her task was done, she effaced herself and committed her erring child into God's keeping. A furtive look of pity, a mute prayer whose fervor was reflected in her eyes, a sign of the cross on Mother Constance's brow, were her only manifestations of tenderness, and she withdrew without saying a word.

Such coldness astonished Adélaide and cut her to the quick. The last bonds which held her to the cloister were broken. No virtue was more alien to her than prudence. She could not understand the hearts of those religious who conceive it their high duty to be always tranquil, whose charity has no warmth, no excess, no apparent tenderness because it is not of the world but of eternity.

III. DESIROUS as she was of keeping under her protection the soul that was so imprudently seeking liberty, the abbess understood immediately that in opposing her maternal wisdom to a will now bent only on escape she would be risking an irreparable breakdown. Since Adélaide was determined to re-enter the world, it became of the gravest importance that she should not do it recklessly and be excommunicated, but should leave the cloister only with the sanction of the Church. Consequently Mother Hermengarde set to work leveling all the obstacles and arranging that she should be dispensed from her vows with the least possible delay. Mother Constance's health and the initial error of her vocation were the justifications for the petition which she addressed to the Congregation of Religious. But the fact that she was a married woman made it incumbent upon those who considered her case to judge it with exceptional caution. The inquiry was long and searching and the formalities dragged on for months. Then, finally, after she had pledged herself faithfully to keep her vow of chastity and never to seek to marry again, she received her letters of secularization.

The moment when her liberty was granted found her very ill. Too weak to make any definite plans, she returned to Paris and having no one else to whom to turn, sought shelter with her brother.

An uncompromising materialist, Maurice Verdon had violently opposed what he termed the "morbid, mystic madness" of his brother-in-law and sister. Little as he understood them, he had been devoted to them. He had admired the perfect harmony of their love. The sudden renunciation of these two fine young beings seemed a sacrilege to him, a crime against life which had so magnificently favored them. He had argued passionately against their decision, for indulgent and conciliatory as he was ordinarily, he was fiercely intolerant in matters of religion. Having made no impression on them, he banished the two bigots from his heart, and forced himself to forget them. He had never replied to the letters which had come to him from Evolayne and from Helmancourt.

Now, when he learned after seven years that his sister was quitting the cloister, all his brotherly affection swept back. By that fact alone she vindicated him, wiped out all his irritation. He was magnanimous enough to level no reproaches against the tired, forsaken, sick woman who was paying with her health and with her happiness for the persistency of her error. As a doctor, he saw that she was threatened

176

with tuberculosis and his first thought was to care for her. He gave her the best he had to offer in his home, forced her to rest and to eat plentifully. He abandoned his irregular, bachelor's habits and came back at set times for meals so that she should not be too much alone. With his easy-going disposition, he was a perfect companion for her.

When he saw that she was less worn out and less feverish, he could not forbear sometimes speaking of the past. From the first, he absolved her from all responsibility. In his eyes she was the victim of a fanatical husband who by persuasion and constraint had forced her into the cloister so that he might enter it himself. And free-thinker that he was, he found in that a splendid pretext for condemning once more the ideas that he had combated all his life. A fine religion it was indeed that consisted in forsaking one's natural duties to bury oneself under a pretense of sacrifice. This much vaunted humility was only another and worse form of human pride. Doubtless it had seemed all too easy to the priest-dominated convert to make a loving wife happy. It was better to shut her up behind a grille and make a virtue for himself of her tears.

Adélaide protested against such accusations. She defended Michel and pointed out the facts. But she realized that her brother was expressing an opinion which would be that of all her former friends and that wherever she appeared, forlorn stave from an incomprehensible shipwreck, she would furnish everyone who took pity on her with arms against the man whom she still loved, and against the Church which she respected. She wanted to disappear, to escape all solicitude and compassion by her absence. The only comfort she desired was from within herself.

Foreseeing that she might be able to leave the convent, she had brought with her upon entering it only the dowry required by the community. The rest she had entrusted to her brother, who had invested it with his own. Seven years' income, compounded, gave her a sufficient sum so that she might care for herself under the best conditions. As soon as she was strong enough to travel, Verdon urged her to go to a warmer climate. Accordingly, she began to make preparations for departure.

On several occasions, she had received letters from Mother Hermengarde but she had not answered them. She made her brother promise never to give her address to Michel if the latter became troubled some day about what had become of her. She wanted all communication between them to be impossible. She needed to be free of every influence so that she might examine in peace what to do with the remainder of her ruined life. This, Maurice fully approved. He wished to see her forget as quickly as possible the man she still had the weakness to love. To him, nothing was irreparably tragic, no sorrow was eternal. Adélaide was still beautiful. He thought a new love would infallibly present itself to her and tear her away from her religious obsessions. Then she would doubtless remarry or take a lover. Already, though he did not say it to her, he believed that irresistible forces of life were at work which little by little would give her back her taste for happiness.

Early in the spring, Adélaide went to Arcachon. And immediately, nature regained such a hold upon her that for a long time she felt unable to think. The sensation of freedom drove everything else from her mind. A sentence kept coming to her from Claudel's *Repos du Septième Jour*. It was from the mouth of the Emperor after he had gone down among the dead:

"Voici que ne sais une chose: je vis! je vis! Ma bouche est fraîche et je sens sur ma main le souffle de mes narines."

It might have been the cry of her own liberation. She had escaped from the stagnant air of the cloister. There were no more grilles about her, no more walls, no more restraint. She was in contact with the world once more, she trod the sand with her bare feet, she touched trees and the flowers, she lifted her face to the moving mass of the wind:

"Je vis! je vis! Ma bouche est fraîche. . . ."

What did it matter if she were alone, forsaken? At certain hours, when the beauty of the world, curling over her like a wave met the rushing waters of her grief, she was almost in ecstasy. The confluence of the two equally powerful currents brought her no consolation, but they rolled her soul dizzily hither and yon. At such times, she was divested of her personality. She was only an echo repeating a babel of words, a thing which vibrated and resounded in a luminous tumult. She took a passionate joy in the outside world, yet she did not find it sufficient. The aptitude which she had for allowing herself to be temporarily distracted from the most poignant grief was, she knew, less a strength than a weakness. Woe to those who are too much alive. Drab, passive natures resign themselves to grief or die of it quickly. But she who had so much and such rich blood in her veins, whose heart was so vulnerable and so responsive, was one of those who can neither live nor die. By not yielding to her suffering, she made it eternal.

Summer came. Tourists, and foreigners, and bathers thronged to the seashore everywhere. Seeking solitude, she returned to Paris in the midst of the heat. Her brother was away and she took a room in a nearly empty hotel. The city, deserted by three-quarters of its population, offered to the occasional pedestrian only parched trees and prospects which shimmered in the sun. Adélaide lived lazily behind closed shutters. Her liberty was already weighing upon her. Her health was better. She had progressed beyond the stimulating period of convalescence when the body that was nearly dead finds itself living once more, and because it had forgotten the taste of life, finds in it a greater savor than formerly it had possessed. The baseless ecstasy which had buoyed her up, the result of her suspension of thought so to speak, came to an end. It was time now to begin the examination of herself and her future.

First of all, she had to face again the essential catastrophe: Michel was lost to her, so completely, so irremediably lost that she envied a widow's grief. Death in depriving them of only the body of their beloved, does away with all risk of misunderstanding and betrayal. The husband for whom they weep remains always as they knew him, always faithful. They can cherish his unchanging image in peace. But that a loved one who is still alive should voluntarily separate from us, should become as an absolute stranger, that is a deprivation which nothing can console. Between Michel her husband, and Father Stéphane there was but a faint resemblance. This Adélaide had realized during their last interview. Yet transformed as he was, she still loved him. As she would have loved him dead or disfigured, she loved him with this new heart which she could not know.

Since she had lost Michel on earth, it was her supreme concern that she should not lose him for eternity. If only she could remain united with him in spirit in this life, perhaps he might be given back to her forever in the next. Her sole hope was to so love him in God that she might forget him for God.

She had tried once to do it, but in vain. While she thought she was losing herself in the infinite, she had succeeded only in falling into the idolatrous worship of a human being. But perhaps that was the result of living a life for which she was wholly unfitted, and at the same time remaining too near to Michel. Now that she had left the cloister, now that no letter, no news, no sign could come to her to fire her love, perhaps, in time, she might be able to resign herself to his absence. Then she would at last be able to find tranquillity and, while remaining free, lead a nun's life in the world, devoting herself to the poor and the sick.

Unfortunately, freed from her husband's influence, she found that she had to resolve afresh and for herself all the problems which he had formerly settled for her. Once more she had to make a difficult choice, decide whether the Catholic faith was indeed the truth for her as well as for Michel, rebuild her personal belief out of the chaos of her mind. She gathered together the books which might be useful to her and at the beginning of September set out for the Vosges where she spent the entire fall, dividing her time between walking and study.

Pascal, the first author to whom she looked for aid, offered her the theory of the game and the wager. The safest thing is to believe in God. Let us wager that He exists. If we lose, we lose nothing. If we have worshiped only a vain image, an illusion, we shall not even know it. We shall have sacrificed to our faith only a contemptible, ephemeral life, and we shall die the dupes of our ignorance. But if the God of whom we have dreamed is waiting for us beyond death, we shall gain eternal reward and eternal love.

This reasoning, logical as it indisputably was, did not please Adélaide. To adopt a religion as one takes out insurance against fire or theft, to devote the same shrewdness to one's spiritual as to one's material concerns, seemed small indeed. If nothing in the world or in one's soul revealed the presence of a Creator, it was nobler to refuse Him one's faith and run the risk of being rejected by Him on the Day of Judgment. A powerful, living God could attach no value to cringing homage offered on the chance of its being right. She did not understand that Pascal's somewhat inglorious wager represented only the first step in encouraging beginners to undertake the greatest of all quests. She went no further with the *Pensées*.

For Descartes, whom she opened next, the idea of God implied the existence of God, as effect supposes cause, since the idea would be inexplicable if one did not admit the object of that idea as its origin and cause.

"The proof of God?" Father Athanase had said to her. "Why, it is within ourselves. Whence would come our desire for perfection, so foreign to us in this world, whence would come our appetite for the unchanging and the eternal when everything before our eyes passes and dies, if it did not reflect a hidden reality, disclosed to us by some inner revelation? More than that, what could be the source of these moral laws to which we submit? Duty cannot come from the world about us, nor from ourselves, since it imposes itself upon us. It is imperative and absolute, it supposes a sovereign good, it supposes God."

Formerly those words had convinced her. Today, she looked upon them with a weary skepticism. Her trampled soul no longer perceived the divine, not even in that universe where so many philosophers had found abounding evidence of it.

Reading Saint Augustine, she felt with him his enchantment before an ordered world whose splendor demanded God. She read the pages in which Saint Thomas proves the existence of a mover, a first intelligence, a first cause, a first Being. Since created things do not exist of themselves, one is led irresistibly to some original Being that exists of itself and is self-sufficient. "Nothing comes from nothing," Bossuet said. If, at the beginning, we placed nothingness, eternally there will be nothing. That which exists today forces us to believe that an eternal God exists.

"All mankind cries out to us that there is a God," said Albertus Magnus. "That which is beautiful gives testimony of a supreme beauty, that which is noble presupposes a Being most noble, that which is pure, a being most pure."

But a desolate heart finds it hard to meditate upon

the splendor of the world, and it does not understand. It rejects the learned arguments which appeal only to reason. Adélaide was blind to the affirmations of the light and consequently she remained enveloped in the darkness of the world: on the one side, dawn, summer, sunshine, the blooming of flowers, the joy of the happy, the justice and gentleness of the good, the greatness of geniuses and heroes; on the other, gloom, winter, whipping storms, the cries of the destitute, the pride of the powerful, war, murder, the cruelty of the strong toward the weak.

Once more, she fell afoul of the problem of evil and suffering. The words of the poet, "Man is a fallen God who remembers the heavens," seemed to her in this connection to be a dazzling truth. They alone reconciled the visible disorder in the world with the goodness and order inherent in it. But could even they explain why universal punishment should be meted out to dumb beasts as well as to sinful man, could they justify that terrible law of survival which allows no life to persist save at the expense of another life?

Adélaide had always possessed a sense of pity and since her grief it had become accentuated. Because she was suffering, she felt in constant communion with all the suffering about her. When she went out for a walk, she noticed the hidden dramas which are unfolded under the most brilliant of suns: the spider and the fly, the cat and the mouse, the hunter and the hunted. "O," she thought, "the remorselessness of it—this constant struggle of life beset by suffering and death. Can it be that God truly wishes it, permits it?"

She soon realized that the barrier which separated her from religion, which prevented her from being a good Christian, was her pessimism. Every Catholic, every believer, shared this fundamental principle: that life, unhappy and helpless as it was, was the most marvelous of gifts. The cry of Lacordaire, "If I were not spirit, I would wish to be matter," was the supreme expression of this passionate worship of existence no matter what the form, what the conditions. From such a feeling, the infinite adoration of the Creator followed naturally; no hardships were as anything compared to the precious gift of being.

Adélaide, on the contrary, felt impelled to consider life as an evil, pain as something irreparable for which no paradise could ever compensate. Moved as she was by all the beauty of the world, she would now have preferred never to have been born. She no longer found happiness except in sleep, when, with the long day ended, she felt her thoughts little by little become heavy, misty, finally cease as the burdensome chariot of her life toppled into the abyss of unconsciousness.

Even as she sought unendingly for certainty, she found it natural enough that the weak, limited spirit of man should be able to grasp only certain relative truths and that he must content himself with them. A sentence of Plato's which she read one day was like a beacon in her night: "From among the systems of human thought, one must choose the best, the surest, and allowing himself to be carried upon it as upon a raft, make his way across life's sea, trusting that he has chosen the right one." But confronted with so many probabilities, often mutually contradictory, her confused, weak, woman's mind hesitated indecisively. All in all, wasn't that which made us incline toward one philosophical system or another, toward negation or toward affirmation, only a personal predilection, as wholly unjustifiable as that which led us to prefer the color blue to the color rose?

Moreover, the Church taught that reason alone does not lead us to faith, which is the free gift of God. Consequently, was there not cause, apparent to all not blinded by prejudice, for seeking faith? Without it, all the power of the reason would attack the mystery of the universe in vain. One's patient effort would be like that of an astronomer trying to number the stars without a telescope. Grace is the instrument whereby the infinite can be understood. Yet it is not sufficient to recognize its utility; one must strive after it, and make oneself worthy of it by prayer and sacrifice.

There, she encountered a new difficulty, the necessity of explaining her own spiritual unsuccess. She recognized that her point of departure was not unassailable, that she had sacrificed her life to Michel and not to God. All her years in the cloister were nothing since they had not been truly offered to her Savior. Not to love God, not to have Him first in her heart, was that not equivalent to condemning herself, to being lost before she started?

This thought came to her in Nice, where she had gone at the beginning of the winter. Not knowing how to use the dragging hours, she had taken the habit of going with her tragic memories to the places intended for leisure and gayety. On this particular day, she was having tea in a little restaurant near the beach, frequented by idlers and where a jazz orchestra was playing. About her were mimosas and violets and smartly dressed women with painted faces and pale, soft hands glittering with jewels. Through the great-paned windows she could see the clear, delicate winter sky, red on the horizon, and the soft blue, almost white, motionless sea. It was in the midst of these surroundings that her heart failed her. The contrast between the charm of what she saw, and the indescribable misery in which she felt herself engulfed was such that she had the vivid, physical impression of hell. Yes, this was the damnation—to have luxury, flowers, a glorious sea spread out before a soul accursed, to have joy offered to one who could no longer participate in it, to have life beckon with its fairest smile to those already stretched in living death. Adélaide listened to the frightful silence within. To all appearances she remained calm, a vague, worldly smile still rested on her lips, but she yielded utterly to temptation, avowed to herself that she was lost. All love was forbidden her, all interchange of thought, all submergence in other beings or in things. She was cut off from Michel, cut off from the people about her, cut off from the peaceful heaven in which God reigned. Never again would she escape from herself. She would be forever prisoner of her perdition. She felt a cold flame devouring her flesh, destroying her form. There remained only a blind, dumb, forgotten creature in which persisted the consciousness of a blasted life.

Later, however, she reacted against her despair and her first concern was to leave Nice whose artificial atmosphere so greatly intensified her unhappiness. At Lyons, where she spent the rest of the winter, she tried to struggle further with the philosophical and religious questions which alone interested her. But with no one to direct her, she wavered aimlessly from one system to another, and her mind, never forceful but clouded now with sorrow, found nothing to which it could cling. This going over and over the same ground availed her nothing. She realized that constant straining of thought leads to madness, that every meditative life needs to take relaxation in some outside activity. The words of Saint Paul: "If I have not charity I am become as sounding brass or as a tinkling cymbal," suggested a new approach to her. Through charity, through the gift of myself, she thought, perhaps I shall reach God more surely than through study and prayer.

But to perform works of charity is not easy. It is not enough to look for misery in order to find it, nor to feel pity for it in order to solace it. Adélaide had difficulty in obtaining the names of some destitute families. And when she had found them, she knew of no way in which to help them except by lavishing, often ill-advisedly, large sums of money which were never sufficient to fill the bottomless pit of their misery. Other hearts, less tender than her own, seemed to have received this gift which she did not possess. She was filled with an immense pity for all unfortunates, but she had had no experience in the slum districts into which she went for the first time. She did not know how to talk to uneducated people. In the presence of the sick, the feeling of her helplessness overwhelmed her. It did not seem to her that she had a right to urge these poor people to resign themselves to their afflictions when her own body had been spared. She could only gaze at them with heart-heavy impotence, turning an imploring, questioning prayer to God while her presence brought no aid.

In one instance only did she feel that her pity was of any avail. This was with a responsive young creature whom she took care of for several months. She was a working girl with a fragile body and a sensitive soul and she was dying of tuberculosis. Her father and brother worked and were forced to leave her alone throughout the day. In that barren, faintly flickering life, the attentions of a kind, beautiful woman, who brought her books and deluged her with gifts and listened tenderly to the recital of her hopes and fears, were an unexpected happiness. Too great a happiness, for it brought its own danger. The girl's gratitude toward her benefactress quickly turned into a hopeless love. She cried when Adélaide stayed a day without coming to see her, and called for her continually.

"Promise me you will never leave me," she would beg. "I will be well by the time you leave Lyons. You will take me with you, won't you?"

Knowing that she could not live, Adélaide acquiesced gently. But the overmastering affection which she had inspired made her realize the limitations of her charity. Suppose she had found this young girl in time and had been able to save her life, what would she have done with her? Their education, ages, background, were too different to permit them ever to continue with one another on any basis of friendly equality.

The child whose dream it had been had no time to discover the utter impossibility of it. Her condition rapidly became grave. Adélaide had her taken to a clinic. One morning, coming to see her, she found her dying and she was alone with her at the end. She saw that poor, racked, plaintive and troubled being become still, slip into the perfect peace from which no suffering could waken her. Death seemed good and compassionate to her. Why was one not permitted to seek it voluntarily, since it alone could cure life which was in itself the cruelest of illnesses?

Among the medicines which Adélaide had purchased for her protégée the morning of her death was a vial of an atropine compound which relieved her when breathing became difficult. As she was on the point of destroying the now useless and dangerous remedy, she hesitated and decided to keep it. The single word "Poison" on the label gave her a sort of security. It seemed pleasant to hold an instrument of deliverance in her hands, if some day she could no longer be able to endure.

Having tried the experiment of devoting herself to others, only to fail there also, she found herself freer and more resourceless than ever.

"What can I do for them?" she thought sadly to herself. "Nothing but give them a little money. I am too lacking in spirituality for my pity to bring consolation. I can't hold out to others a God in whom I am not sure that I myself believe, nor peace which I don't possess, nor the heart that belongs irrevocably to another."

She turned a considerable sum over to the sisters of Saint Vincent de Paul for the families in which she had been interested, and certain that the funds would be more wisely distributed than she ever could do it, she departed for the mountains.

IV.

A YEAR had rolled by since she had left the cloister, a fruitless year. Neither in thought nor in action had she been able to turn toward God. She no longer performed her religious duties except to the extent required in order to remain within the pale of the Church of which Michel was a part. But the idea of religion obsessed her without ever giving her comfort; it seemed plausible or inconceivable as grief lay more or less heavily upon her.

As she lost hope of finding a solution, she relaxed her discipline over herself, and instead of resisting her love, she yielded to it. Michel was always at her side and their conversations went on and on until reality, stripping away the illusion of his presence, cut into her like a knife. The thought that he was living but lost to her forever, made her senses reel. She no longer accepted the idea of absolute separation, of wholly forgetting him.

It was cruel, this silence always surrounding her, this absence of all communication with anyone. She surprised herself sometimes, when she was alone in the woods or at night, by speaking out loud to make sure that the seal upon her mouth was not that of death. Truth to tell, it was only her own wish which kept her cut off from people. In the hotels where she stayed, she invariably aroused sympathetic curiosity. Her beauty marked her out even more than her solitariness. Advances were made to her but invariably she withdrew. Sometimes she felt drawn to certain individuals: elderly ladies with a kindly manner, or sick young girls. Occasionally after a chance meeting she entered into brief conversation. But at the first hint of intimacy she took fright at the thought that they might question her, might seek to penetrate the mystery of her life. Her sorrow seemed too exceptional to her ever to be avowed. She was as ashamed of it as she might have been of a crime and trembled for fear it would be discovered. As soon as she became too well known in one hotel, she would leave. In this manner she stayed at several places in Haute-Savoie and at length stopped at a *pension de famille* located on a slope of the Voyrons.

The countryside was magnificent. The meadows gradually dipping away under sun and shadow alternated with solemn forests where on the brightest days one walked in a fresh, green half-light.

One afternoon, having climbed to the top of the Voyrons, Adélaide was caught in a violent storm which forced her to seek shelter for several hours in an abandoned inn. When she was able to set out again, fog enveloped the mountain. She could not find her path and she was forced to picked her way at random down the wet and for the most part, precipitous slopes, falling heavily several times. It was already growing dark when she found herself plodding through the mud of the bottom. With great difficulty she reached the forest-covered plain. There, while she was struggling to get her bearings, night set in in earnest. It was impossible to find a landmark. The air grew cold. From time to time gusts of wind shook the tree-tops, sending down a deluge of rain. Adélaide groped on, with her arms stretched before her to fend against the trees she could no longer see. Her feet stumbled over the projecting roots of the firs. Before long she stopped, a prisoner of the night, too tired to continue the hopeless struggle. Finding a stump, she sat down upon it.

There was nothing to do but to stay there until daybreak, scarcely a pleasant prospect. She had set out with no other wrap than a long woolen scarf, now so saturated with dampness that the touch of it made her shiver. Her shoes were masses of sticky mud, her wet stockings clung icily to her legs. She had not eaten since noon and she was cold and hungry. Her physical exhaustion led her to take the disagreeable situation tragically. Certainly there was no creature on earth whose abandonment was comparable to her own. A horse, a dog, a sheep, no matter what domestic animal, has a master who looks for it when it is lost, but she, a human being, could lose herself in the depths of the woods, could be cold and afraid, without anyone in the world troubling. She might die there that night. Her body would be found sooner or later, but with only her name as a clew to go by, no one would be able to discover what her place in the world had been, no one would be able to notify him who was still her husband.

Her husband! She sobbed, and her tears overflowed. Accustomed to suffering through Michel, she blamed him for all the discomforts which she was enduring. One would have said that in closing his heart to her, Michel had purposedly driven her out into the storm and darkness. It was because he had abandoned her that she was poor and destitute and homeless, and the words of Lear came to her lips:

"O, O, 'tis foul!"

Then, suddenly, through the whistling of the wind and the groaning of the trees, she heard a voice calling from a distance. Doubtless someone well beloved was lost and family and friends were searching anxiously. She might be able to take advantage of a mistake which would enable her to find her way back to her hotel and to bed. She cried out in turn with all her strength, and was heard. The voice of a man called at intervals, coming closer, guided by her replies. Soon through the trees she made out the gleam of a flashlight moving to and fro, piercing the darkness. Then the call came again:

"Where are you?"

At the same time the pencil of light picked her

out, shone in her eyes. Then the stranger turned its rays on himself so that she might see him and not be afraid. In just the same way on the winter evening when Michel had taken her to the gate of the abbey of Helmancourt, before leaving her forever, he had gazed at her face in the darkness, then turned the light upon himself so that she might contemplate his own. And Adélaide, deluded by the similarity of the two scenes, thought she recognized the beloved face and figure. A cry escaped her:

"Michel!"

Then another cry, stronger still:

"Are you living or dead?"

Suddenly trembling, the voice answered:

"Don't be afraid, Madame Adrian, I am Bernard Vallin from your hotel."

By chance she had heard the name of this young man who for the last few days had been taking his meals at a table near her own. He looked a little like Michel: the same type of physique, the same cast of features. Fatigue and emotion had deceived her into taking one for the other. He, however, thought that she was sick or hurt and that she was delirious. He knelt down beside her and flashed his light on her face, which was ghastly pale but otherwise seemed normal. He felt her wet clothing, took off her damp scarf and wrapped her in a topcoat which he had over his arm. Then he lifted a little flask to her lips. She took a swallow of brandy and its strength warmed her. She murmured a feeble thank you. Then he questioned her anxiously.

"Are you hurt, Madame? Can you walk to the hotel? It's not far, scarcely a quarter of a mile. Or do you want me to get help?"

She reassured him. She was not sick, only stiff from sitting in the cold and damp.

As soon as she had gone a few steps, leaning on his arm, she felt better. He guided her solicitously, pointing out the slightest obstacles: roots of trees, broken branches, stones. Finally they reached the path. Not until then did she think of the disappointment which her companion must be feeling at finding a stranger instead of the friend for whom he was searching.

"But weren't you looking for someone?" she said.

"Why, yes, you," he said, to her immense surprise. "Everybody in the hotel has been worried. You were not at your place at dinner. The proprietress thought that you had gone to the top of the Voyrons because you asked her yesterday how far it was. When night came on, we were afraid something had happened to you. All the men set out with lights in different directions and I had the great good luck to find you."

She was touched by so much thoughtfulness.

"How good and kind of all of you," she said.

Downstairs in the hotel, all the guests were waiting for her. She felt as if she were coming back to a big family where she had left only strangers. The incident drew her immediately into the circle.

"I am too well known," she thought, "I must leave."

Nevertheless, she stayed. The sympathy which everyone showed her was sweet. She no longer passed among the living like a wraith whom no one seemed to notice. Faces lit up at the sight of her, hands stretched out toward her own. Every day now she exchanged a few words, a few ideas with human beings, and these conversations, superficial as they were, soothed her sadness. Among all her friends, the closest was Bernard Vallin, and the rights which he had to her gratitude lent their relationship a sort of intimacy. She felt that he was interested in her in a different way from the others, and that it was he who, on the evening of the storm, had first become anxious about her and that without him the rest would have gone tranquilly to sleep without thinking of looking for her. Now, he watched over her constantly. If she was late for dinner, he waited for her at the door of the hotel and greeted her with a sigh of relief. When he saw her setting out, he cautioned her:

"Don't get lost!"

He warned her when the weather looked dubious, told her where to go for the most beautiful walks. Since he knew the country well—he had been a frequent visitor at the pension—he proposed one day that he should show her the way to a distant forest to which she had not yet visited. He seemed so unhappy, and so terrified as he waited for her reply, that she did not have the courage to refuse. Thereafter, they set out frequently together.

She did not deceive herself about the nature of his sentiments toward her, but she closed her eyes to the dangers. After so many years of humiliation, it was pleasant to exist for someone again. She began to take renewed pride in her beauty when she saw it reflected with adoration in the eyes which looked upon her and which had in them something of Michel's expression. This quickening of his heart toward her gave a warmth to her life, a value to the otherwise empty days. She was drawn by Bernard's lack of self-consciousness and by his spontaneity, so rare in men. He was an unbeliever, but he had a religious temperament that, if not concerned in seeking ultimate truth, was ceaselessly concerned in plumbing the significance of his own discontent. Their common love of nature was a bond between them. Their friendship grew apace.

In the course of their long conversations, Bernard spoke freely about himself and about his family. He was thirty-five, he lived in Paris with his mother. He had three married sisters of whom he was very fond and he confessed that he was happy only in the company of women. Cautious, Adélaide revealed nothing of her past. He dared not seek her confidences from her, and limited himself to trying to fill in the vague bits of information concerning her life which she dropped by chance as they talked.

"When I was living in Paris," she said one day.

Quickly he asked:

"You no longer live there?"

She replied in the negative without going into it further. Another time, he thought he caught a clew in a different direction. She said:

"At Lyons this winter . . ."

"Then you live in Lyons?" he asked again.

"No," she said, "I have been traveling about."

At the hotel, the mail arrived every day at luncheon time. He noticed with amazement that she never received any letters, apparently never expected any, for the distribution which preoccupied everyone else left her indifferent. It was in this way that he became convinced that she had neither home, nor family, nor friends, and that the lot of this woman, who seemed made for all the tenderness and happiness in the world, must be a bitter one.

The discovery made her even dearer to him. Her beauty seemed more moving because it was surrounded by secret sorrow. The attraction of her face became less to his imaginative spirit than that of her mysterious life. With the love which she inspired in him there thus came to be mingled a deep concern of which she could not fail to be conscious.

One evening after dinner while taking a little walk along the road, as they had fallen into the habit of doing, Bernard intentionally brought up the subject of loneliness. He said that he liked it, if it did not continue for too long. He sought it sometimes to refresh his spirit just as, in summer, he sought nature. But after a time it seemed depressing and cruel to him. If he should lose his mother, he would marry. He would not be able to bear living face to face with himself perpetually, always going back to a home where no one was waiting for him.

"One becomes accustomed to it, as one does to absence or exile or prison or anything here on earth," she answered. "It is unbelievable, man's resistance to everything fate can do. There is no torment strong enough to kill. Our heart suffers, bleeds, but it endures without breaking."

Bernard interrupted her generalities and came back to his point of departure.

"You live absolutely alone?"

"Yes, since . . ."

She was going to say: "Since I left the convent," but she caught herself and finished:

"Since I have been a widow."

First discovery! For him a supremely important one. She was a widow and consequently she was free. He asked her how long that had been.

"A year," she answered.

He excused himself for having by his questions called up so recent a sorrow, but at the same time he glanced with surprise at her dress which was of unbleached muslin with huge orange flowers. She did not wish him to think her untruthful, to think that she was inventing an imaginary grief in order to make herself interesting.

"I put it badly," she went on. "I am truly a widow, but I am the widow of a man who is still alive. I am not sure that it isn't easier to lose someone through death than through abandonment."

"Abandonment!" He repeated the word with an amazement which was very sweet to her ears.

"Ah, Michel," she thought, "see how astonished he is at what you have done. I don't seem to him to be a woman whom one would renounce."

And in truth for Bernard she was the ideal, the one perfect, desirable being of whom he could never tire. He was filled with indignation at the man who had had such a wife and had been able to forsake her. He must have been contemptible, wholly unworthy of her. And yet she seemed to love him.

"Why do you suppose it is," she went on, "that two hearts can never feel equally toward one another? In every couple there is only one who truly loves, and that is the woman."

He was about to protest warmly, when he saw that she was crying. Then he took her hand, gently, affectionately. Very softly he said, "My dear friend." And something began between them: a tenderness, an intimacy made of trust, and pity, and desire. They were surrounded by a murmur as of music, through which they heard each other magically, in a dream.

The days which followed were precious to Adélaide, for in them she found the somewhat troubled sweetness of being able to lament freely to one who loved her. Her sorrow was no longer a stagnant pool within her, but an unquenchable torrent which had at last found an opening and was overflowing into another heart. Bernard proved himself a magnanimous confidant. Patiently he allowed himself to be wounded by her, listened to her talk about Michel without giving any sign of his jealousy. But try as love will to be thoughtless of itself, it is forever selfish and interested. When a man sees a woman whom he desires, suffering, he may pretend that he is forgetting himself for her. But in his pity, he is thinking only of the moment when she will be his to console.

Unconsciously cruel, Adélaide accepted Bernard's love, played with it, without having any intention of fulfilling it. She thought that she could postpone the avowal of it indefinitely. Confident of her security, she courted danger in their conversations and in their long hours alone together. The walks which she took with Bernard at sunset lasted now until after nightfall. One evening, as he was leaving her at the door of her room, he took her in his arms.

Immediately she slipped away and she was pleased with her coolness that it made so little demand on either her courage or her strength of will. Not until a few moments later did she become conscious of the physical sensation of the kiss which had brushed her lips. The emotion, slow in starting, swelled and deepened until it shook every part of her being, until she was like a woman gone mad, calling in misery not for Bernard, not for any definite person, but for love, love only. O, to be given any tenderness, to feel any heart close against her own! Standing on her balcony, alone, looking into the glorious night, she consented to this first lapse, and even then she foresaw all that might follow. The memory of Michel never left her, but at that moment it was no longer a safeguard. An instinct for vengeance made her want to lose all hope of salvation, wanted him to know it, so that, wounded in his conscience if not in his heart, he might realize that in abandoning her he had brought damnation on her.

Next morning, however, when sleep had cleared the confusion in her heart and brain, when she examined herself under the pure eyes of the day, she realized that she must seize the first opportunity to flee the dangers with which she had trifled so complacently. Her soul was too noble to yield to this impulse for degradation which sooner or later tempts everyone whose ideal of life has been frustrated. The fact that for a moment she had desired an affair, revealed her weakness. The disillusionment preceded the experience. Perhaps she was already tired of the faint joys which she had tasted. The habit of sorrow made all renunciation easy. Besides, she felt pity for Bernard who loved her sincerely, while to her he was only an unreal image. It was better to put an end as quickly as possible to this game in which he risked breaking his heart.

The following day, she accepted his offer to go and get some books for her in Geneva. As soon as he was gone, she packed her trunk, called for a taxi and paid her bill. She left for Bernard only a word of farewell, vague and courteous, and no address.

Again, she went from place to place; she visited Chambéry, Annecy, took a trip around Lake Bourget. She missed Bernard, though for his friendship only, and her loneliness seemed harder than ever to bear after its momentary interruption. September was beginning. Fall was near. She had no plans for winter and she could not decide upon any, knowing well that she was unfitted for any kind of social or charitable activity. Why, after all, was she always searching for some cause, some great task, when she knew that the lives of so many are futile, when so many people succeed in living mechanically, without any ideals, or definite beliefs or duties? Toward middle age, most women find themselves facing an empty future: mothers whose children have married, women whose beauty is fading and who no longer find it easy to please, spinsters who have not found love and for whom the long wait is at an end. They all resign themselves. Household affairs, keeping in touch with friends and relations help them to pass the time, prevent them from perceiving that they are accomplishing nothing here on earth. Adélaide could go back to Paris. She loved books and music enough to find some interesting things to do. She would still suffer, but little by little the attacks would become further apart and she would wait for old age and death. This program of submission, wise by and large, which all the conquered of the world accept, revolted her as a treason.

"I was made for other things," she told herself, "for a single love, for a single person."

But Michel had abandoned her and each day she was losing him a little more. She no longer remembered the exact timbre of his voice or the expression of his face, only his name and the overwhelming fact of his life.

One night, after she had brooded too long over those happy hours now lost to her forever, the temptation came to put an end to her torture. With the thought, a profound silence seemed to reign within her. Grief threw its crushing weight into the balance. Her flesh and heart yielded, besought eternal sleep. But as Adélaide's hand touched the carefully treasured vial of atropine, her soul drew back in horror. Softly it protested, opposing the patience of the weak to that terrible desire, arguing timidly: "Later, there is plenty of time yet. . . ." Thus it gained one second after another, staved off the fatal act until fear brought the taste for life sweeping back over all her being.

Then, still trembling from the danger she had run, Adélaide burst into tears and no longer being able to pray cried out to Michel as toward her savior. And that, in truth, was what he was for her. She knew finally, after her long trial, that she believed only in him. Away from his influence, she was but a sick, troubled thing. With no thought of reëstablishing the bonds which had been broken forever, she felt that her long sacrifice had given her the right to go back to him, to ask his help, to tell him of her unhappiness. He alone could discover its cause, could discern its gravity, could find a remedy for it. The thought that she might perhaps destroy his peace did not deter her. It was overwhelmingly evident to her that their two lots could not be separated. She had suffered in order to give him to God, he could suffer now in order to save her. She did not foresee the dangers of such a return, nor the limits which the memory of their former love would impose upon the charity of the priest. As soon as she had realized in her mind the fact that she might rejoin him, everything was said. Hope, like an irresistible wave, carried her to Michel. She set out, reached Paris, spent a single night there, set out again and on a beautiful, quiet evening, leaning out of the window of her train, she saw the two towers of the abbey glinting in the sun.

At the *Hôtellerie de la Drachme Perdue* she recognized no one. The proprietors and the staff were new. Even in this place where life changes so little, many things might have happened. Sometimes the monks were sent away on missions, or into other monasteries. Perhaps Michel was away, or sick. At dinner she questioned the innkeeper.

"Is Dom Wilfred still the abbot?"

"Still!"

"And is Father Athanase still here?"

"Yes."

She named several other monks and received the same reply. Then with pounding heart she asked:

"And Father Stéphane?"

The innkeeper exclaimed:

"Oh, yes indeed; he is the one who was married. He preached last Sunday. He speaks well. You seem to know all the fathers, Madame."

"Almost all," she said carelessly. "I once spent several years here."

She fell silent. Her heart was full of joy and tenderness and fright.

PART THREE

I. THAT night, Adélaide scorned sleep, forcing herself to stay awake so that she should lose nothing of the hours which she was living. It is not the greatness of an event which determines the amount of happiness or sorrow which it brings. The intensity of the emotion depends upon our changeable hearts which, unreasonably exacting or unreasonably humble, sometimes reject the finest gifts of fate, sometimes make a treasure of a trifling favor. The younger we are, the more wanton are we with that which is given us. Those who have grown mature and have suffered much can draw infinite pleasure from a little cause. Because she had endured abandonment and homelessness and loneliness, Adélaide appreciated the preciousness of her beloved's presence, of the bliss which comes with a look, a word, a touch of the hands exchanged between two lovers separated by duty. Because she had thrown away so many priceless hours, she was determined to relish to the full the moment, now so near, when Michel would be given back to her. O, how she would hold to it! She was already preparing herself for it in the still darkness, living it in advance so that she might leave nothing to chance. She anticipated both a great joy and a great light. Those brief few minutes must make up for the past, must guide her future. But in order that it might do so, her heart had to be calm, her mind clear and cool and tensely alert. She would have to catch at a glance whatever sign there showed on Michel's face of his remaining love for her. Simultaneously she would have to receive and to give: to receive his soul and to give him hers. Her life depended on that first look, that first contact. Through a mutual effort of confidence, they would have to banish all misunderstandings, all the results of their separation, re-create between themselves the intimacy of marriage. When Michel had understood her, he would assume his old authority over her. He would say: "Here are the causes of the trouble, here is the remedy, here is what you must do, here is what you must think." And she would have only to obey. Life would become easy once more.

Obscurely she realized that the happiness of their reunion could never equal in its fullness the joy of this moment in which she was picturing it to herself. Consequently she yearned to prolong it. When morning came, instead of going up to the abbey for high Mass, she decided to put off until afternoon her meeting with Michel. She wandered about the countryside, fleeing then seeking the abbey by turns. When she was in the woods and was unable to catch sight

214

of it for a few minutes, she hastened to find some open spot where she could contemplate its towering mass of stone. She gazed at it almost as if it were a face. She thought that Michel was living there, that perhaps at this very moment he was praying for her. She took a delight tinged with malice from the thought that he was ignorant of her return, was perhaps worrying about her at that moment when she was so happy.

Immediately after luncheon she went up to her room and began her preparations. First of all, she studied herself for a long time in the mirror, seeking the traces of the years in her face. Minute as was her scrutiny, it revealed only the most meager of blemishes. The line about her mouth had deepened. On certain days, when she was tired, it made her look older. But today, in conjunction with the smoldering languor of her eyes, that pathetic line only emphasized the emotional character of her features. She noticed a few rough places on her cheeks and temples, and after massaging her face, she used a little rouge. She anticipated that Michel would at least take her hands, so she bestowed infinite care upon them. Then a thought occurred to her which chilled her:

"He is a priest, he will no longer think of me as a woman!"

Fearing to displease him, she wiped off almost all the cosmetics. She chose a simple dress of gray and black printed crêpe de Chine, a short black satin jacket and a velvet béret with a long embroidered veil. She put on no jewels, no ornaments.

Her toilet finished, she wrote a note for her husband. Then her feelings underwent a change; she became anxious, feverish, finally fell into utter panic as she entered the abbey and perceived that vespers were almost over and that only a few minutes separated her from her longed-for meeting. In her weakness and her fright she was tempted to flee and put off seeing Michel until the next day. But then the office came to an end and the monks, leaving the choir, filed slowly through the door of the cloister. She was terrified not to be able to recognize from the distance the figure which she sought. The thought suddenly came back to her that perhaps Michel was away, and immediately she was in anguish. The waiting which she had savored so lovingly a little while before, became a torment and she doubted whether she could bear it for another day, even another hour. Hastily she left the church and made her way to the little book-room where tourists bought holy pictures and books and rosaries. She approached the brother porter and asked for Father Stéphane, trembling in the fear of a negative reply. But without hesitation the brother merely repeated:

"Father Stéphane? Very well, I'll tell him."

She held out the note she had written. Then he ushered her into one of the numerous reception rooms where many a time she had waited for Father

Athanase. They were all alike. All were of the same dimensions, all were furnished identically with a large round table and a few chairs. A crucifix and, opposite it, a portrait of the Pope were the only decorations on the walls. On the plain glass panes of the windows, set very high, the shadow of the trees moved in every breath of wind.

Left alone in the room, Adélaide waited, she could not have told how long. Standing, with her eyes fixed on the door, her mind no longer functioned. She listened to the pounding of her heart, to life beating on within her, until that dull tumult was drowned in the sound of approaching footsteps. The door opened. The miracle, so constantly dreamed of, came to pass. The emptiness before her exploded, was shattered into pieces by a presence which suddenly filled it to the exclusion of everything else. But of that wonderful instant of meeting, of that long awaited happiness, she could grasp almost nothing. Emotions too deeply felt are as violent and as confused in their rapidity as those called up by an accident. She was like a person struck by a bullet, before whom the abyss opens and who, before death, catches at random one or two last fleeting, broken impressions. She heard the dear voice, very near to her, repeating her name several times. She saw the unforgettable face bending toward hers, and her eyes dropped to his monk's robe, so black, so somber; then they closed. She did not read Michel's thoughts in his face, she did not understand the words he spoke, she did not receive his soul. Everything escaped her, including her own joy. Her senses, dazed by the emotion which they were undergoing, grew faint and let slip their delight. She did not lose consciousness, but a sort of dizzy prostration engulfed her. Already, with the speed of lightning, the instant had passed.

A little later, when she returned to earth and to a realization of what was taking place, she heard the familiar voice once more, but this time it was no longer so close. She opened her eyes. They were seated opposite one another. The table separated them. And this was her first grief, that Michel, her husband, received her thus like a stranger and kept her at a distance. Nevertheless she bowed humbly to his will. The sweetness of his presence made up for any disappointment. He was there. She looked at him, not fixedly, but with little quick glances, as one drinks an overstrong liqueur, drop by drop, pausing between each sip. Every glance recovered some lost trait of his face: first, the eyes that were so clear, with their long, thick lashes falling like a veil of gentle rain over their depths; then the straight, somewhat thick nose with that slight furrow close to the nostrils which emotion always put there; the chin, cleft in the middle; the rather square jaw; the curving mouth; the charming smile. He looked older. His hair was grayer and now receded from his forehead which was more deeply lined. But his face as a whole gave the impression of being less severe, less taut. She loved him even better this way than as he had been in her memory. She found him changed without being able to explain to herself why. Very probably it was less because of the years than because of the extraordinary joy which shone in his eyes—a joy such as no worldly pleasures give, but which she had seen before transforming Father Athanase's stern features. As if to explain this joy, though it came from quite another source, Michel exclaimed:

"I am very happy, Adé. It is you at last. We are together again."

She repeated:

"Together again."

In those two words were summed up for her all the delights of heaven. She leaned forward, her hands stretched out to him.

"Is it possible," she thought, "that this man once held me in his arms! How cold I must have been! I received his caresses, now I should die if he were to kiss me. Why hasn't he kissed me? Hasn't he even wanted to? Doesn't seeing me remind him of our happiness together? Has he such mastery over his thoughts that he has forgotten what he has renounced?"

Her fierce longing for the past, the bitter charm of the present, absorbed her so completely that she did not care whether Michel spoke. But he knew the dangers of silence and he did not wish to let her lose herself in reveries that would be dangerous for both of them. He went on, authoritatively:

"You have acted very wrongly toward me, Adé! How could you have let me go without news of you? Death could not have separated us more completely than that unbending will of yours. I should not have thought you capable of such cruelty."

That bold reproach, when he had so much to answer for regarding her, was sweet to her; she was pleased with its injustice, for the fact that he expressed a grievance against her proved that he still felt that he held certain rights over her.

"I thought," she said, excusing herself, "that it was best not to disturb your work."

"My work is to share my joy with others, and above all with the soul for which I am responsible before God."

"You are happy, then?"

"One is always happy when one has found the light. But if anything could have destroyed the ineffable peace which our Master grants as soon as we give ourselves to Him, it would have been the thought that you did not share it. I cannot pursue my way in contentment unless you follow me. How many prayers I have sent up to heaven for you! Never for a moment has the memory of you been absent from me. At work, in meditation, at the altar, the question so long unanswered has been always in my heart: 'Where is my poor child?' "

Adélaide did not quite know whether these words which seemed tender were those which she had expected or not. Still dazed by the ecstasy of being with Michel again, she was not lucid enough to comprehend their real significance. She found them at once delectable and unsatisfying, and she exerted herself primarily to remember them exactly so that she might analyze them later.

"Are you really so much to be pitied?" she murmured. "I thought that God was with you."

"He was. None other than that supreme Friend could have helped me to endure your disappearance, the total silence, the absolute ignorance of what had become of you."

"But I," she groaned, "I was alone."

"No," he said. "The same Friend was with you who was with me, present though invisible."

Such a light shone in his eyes that she was startled. O, to submit, to believe humbly as he believed! Why did it have to be that the truth which seemed obvious to him was hidden or shrouded in doubt for her? Perhaps if he would lay his hand on hers their hearts would cease to be so divided, would be merged in the same adoration. She gazed attentively at that long, big-jointed hand which was not beautiful, perhaps, but which she loved. She brushed it lightly with her fingers. Michel appeared not to notice her caress, but a moment later he crossed his arms in the wide sleeves of his habit in the customary manner of the monk.

"Let us begin at the very beginning," he said. "There is a gap of eighteen months between us to be filled. Where have you been?"

"A little everywhere; the last few months in Haute-Savoie."

"What took you there?"

"Nothing in particular. What difference did it make where I was?"

"I don't quite understand. Remember, Adé, I have known nothing of you for a very long time. One day the astounding news came to me that you had asked to be relieved of your vows. I was told that you were ill, that the atmosphere of the cloister did not agree with you. I often asked other explanations but they were refused me. That is the only time obedience has seemed cruel indeed. About six months ago the Father Abbot gave me permission to write to you. Mother Hermengarde had requested it of him because she had had no news of you and she was worried. I wrote you several letters in Maurice's care, asking him to forward them to you. He answered that he would not do it, that you needed rest and were traveling."

"Yes, I was never long at one address. I lived in Arcachon, in the Vosges, in Nice, in Lyons, here and there, any place."

"By doctor's orders, I presume?"

"At first, yes, but then I gave up trying to care for myself. I wanted death, but it would not take me."

"How did you occupy yourself, leading such a life?"

"I read a great deal, I studied. I thought of you. I wept a great deal, too."

With enormous pity, mingled with severity, he said:

"That is not the way of salvation."

"What does it matter!" she cried bitterly, "provided you find yours."

She wished immediately that she had not said it. Here at a time when after all their sorrow they should have had only indulgence and forgiveness one for the other, she was the first to rekindle the flame which always threatens to turn lovers into enemies. Michel, more patient than she because he did not love as she did, let drop the arrow with which she had wounded him. Attentively as she watched his face, she saw no sign of suffering or anger. Whether it was that he had acquired the perfect mastery over himself toward which all ascetics aspire, or whether he had become invulnerable, outwardly he remained perfectly calm. One single indication there was that perhaps she had struck deep: a more intense joy, a more brilliant light shone in his eyes. To the saints all humiliation is pleasing. He was silent a moment, then he went on with his questioning.

"You didn't know that I had written to Maurice?"

"No, it was agreed that he would never speak to me about you."

"I prefer that. I feared for a moment that you might have dictated his last letter which hurt me cruelly."

"What did he say?"

"He accused me of having sacrificed you, having tortured you, then he went on to say: content yourself with the assurance that Adé is alive, and leave her alone. Since you believe in the effectiveness of prayer, at least implore heaven that she may forget you and take a lover. It is the best thing that could happen."

"Yes," murmured Adélaide, "that is so."

This time Michel started.

"Can it be that you approve of that suggestion?"

She gave a discouraged smile.

"Another love would have cured me."

"If it was question of a cure, why did you not turn to Him who is able to console and save?"

"Others, perhaps, but not me."

She took a certain grim pleasure in at last seeing Michel's consternation over the misery she was revealing to him. Nevertheless, with a great effort, he succeeded in controlling himself.

"We are straying from the point," he said, "we are losing ourselves in non-essentials. I cannot understand you because you have not yet explained anything to me. I must first know why you left Helmancourt, and then tell me as fully as you can about your

224

spiritual life since your departure. I am sure, Adé, that you will keep nothing from me."

She had prepared herself only for those unforced confidences which one exchanges hand in hand, eyes in eyes, heart against heart. The space which separated them, slight as it was, was not conducive to revelation. When bodies are kept apart, souls, ardently as they may seek each other, cannot join. Moreover, far from helping her to unburden herself, Michel had just created a new difficulty by turning his eyes away from her. His elbow on the table, covering his face with his hand, he had instinctively taken the attitude of the confessor with a penitent. She was chilled that he should thus cut himself off from her, should be only a judge, hidden, inaccessible, weighing her slightest words in order to pronounce judgment.

With difficulty she began to speak.

"I left Helmancourt because I realized that I had been mistaken about my vocation. It may seem strange to you that I should make the discovery only after seven years. But one can live a long time under the spell of an illusion which a single day may dissipate, leaving only emptiness behind it. Why? No one can say. It's like the soap bubble that bursts, not because it has been pricked, but simply because its limited life is over. Eventually I came to understand my error. God had not called me. The cloister was a prison to me. I fled. I studied, meditated, prayed. I tried to lead a good and useful life in the world. I took care of the poor and the sick. In that too I failed. I didn't know how to practice charity. I had not received the gift which enables one to console others. A heart full of pity is not enough, and instead of gaining some sort of certainty, I lost that which I thought I had. Now, I no longer even have faith."

How ineffectual her words were! How far they came from explaining her long struggle and her defeat! Only when one is alone does grief weigh down upon the soul with all its force. The presence of one who is beloved, or even of a stranger, lightens it. At the moment when Adélaide wanted to express the whole burden of her distress, she no longer felt it, and her misery being only a memory, she did not succeed in making it a reality for him who was listening. Consequently he remained unmoved.

"I recognize my impulsive Adé," he said with a compassion that was almost gay. "Feminine, too feminine; all contrasts and changes of heart, each one of which she thinks is definitive. The first serious temptation vanquished you. You wished to be constantly sustained by grace. You were not able to bear finding yourself in darkness for a little while, and unhappy."

"You are wrong," she said proudly. "In leaving Helmancourt I did not yield, as you seem to think, to any passing impulse of rebellion. I believed that no sincere person should follow a way of life which did not correspond to his highest aspirations and his beliefs. It required more courage than cowardice for me to leave the cloister. Liberty was no boon to me. I can endure unhappiness, for it is only through it that anything is ever achieved, but despair is futile, and I had reached despair."

To her great surprise, that grave confession to which Michel should have replied with a rush of sympathy, troubled him not at all. At the first summons, no happy individual is inclined to make the effort necessary to leave the shining peaks where he dwells and go down into the shades where his fellow man is struggling. The most constant, the most loving charity does not descend beyond a certain zone of sorrow. What is sickness for one whose body has never known weakness or faltering? What is death for the young heart pulsing with life? The priest in his certainty knows that there are individuals who fall into absolute disbelief, into total rebellion, but so rare, so exceptional a crime has little reality for him. In his eyes, despair is only a word which the worldly are likely to use without true significance, as when they say: "I am bored to death."

"You are exaggerating the importance of your difficulty," Father Stéphane replied posedly. "Nothing in your state of mind seems to me truly grave or irremediable . . . unless . . ."

His voice broke a little. He finished in a lower tone:

"Unless you have dishonored your soul through mortal sin."

That was his only real concern. He had lost the habit of being much moved at the sight of suffering, knowing that it was salutary. As a monk he dreaded only sin, and he trembled for fear Adélaide, after her spiritual crisis, with no one to guide her, with thenceforth no aim and no duties in life, might have sought happiness in forbidden pleasure. As her reply was slow in coming, as she seemed to hesitate before a difficult confession, he went on in still greater anguish:

"You can tell me everything, Adé. Whatever your faults have been, I shall take my share of the responsibility for them and I shall not condemn you."

She was happy, indescribably happy at the torment which she was causing him and which she erroneously ascribed to the jealousy of the man rather than to that of the priest. She reassured him, not without pride:

"There is no stain on my life." And she added tenderly, "You alone have kept me from it."

"Not I," he interposed. "God!"

"You alone," she insisted. "If it had not been for you, perhaps I would have accepted the love which was offered to me a short time ago, a beautiful love. But in yielding to it, I would have had to separate myself from you morally. I would have had to close the door upon the past, to banish the memory of you from my heart, renounce even this hour which is given to me today. I could not do that."

Then, once more, he looked at her and at his glance her soul became like a house which has been closed during a long winter and whose windows are opened one by one to the bright spring sun. Yet she realized that this feeling of solace was only a passing, illusory thing. Her grief still persisted within her. She forced herself not to lose sight of the darkness from which she was emerging, and into which she would fall again.

"Take pity on me," she pleaded. "I was desolate, so uncertain of my way."

"Then why have you come back here?" he asked gently.

"How can I know? Because I was suffering more than I could bear, because from turning the same ideas over and over in my mind I no longer understood anything, because I thought that you would help me perhaps."

"Because you hoped," he said triumphantly. "Admit it. As in every being who is threatened, danger made you realize that you must turn to something stronger than yourself, and God sent you to me who was calling you. This very morning I finished a novena—the third since your departure—for you to be given back to me. Imagine my thanksgiving when the brother porter brought me your note. Can you not see how Divine Providence has manifested itself in the fact that you have come?"

"It might just as well be called coincidence or chance. Three novenas, you said? The first two were unavailing."

"Jesus at first repulsed the Canaanite woman. He wishes to test our faith. But the prayer that perseveres never fails."

"For you everything is a miracle!"

"For me, and for all who know how to see. Open your eyes, Adé. The joy which you are seeking is here before you; you have only to stretch out your hand."

"Joy," she said. "I knew it once when I was with you, and I would find it again if I could live near you and see you every day."

He started slightly in alarm, but she scarcely noticed.

"I am speaking of the only true joy," he corrected her firmly, "the joy which our Master reserves for His elect."

But she had ceased abruptly to take an interest in the problem of her destiny. This discussion which should have been so intimate, so beautiful, went astray because when the opportune moment came neither could find the precise, profound words which alone go to the root of misunderstandings and banish them. She no longer thought of anything but her love and one little detail preoccupied her.

"I am not one of the elect," she said musingly. "To tell the truth, I am glad not to be a nun to you any more, because now you call me Adé, as you used to. I hardly know what to call you. Should I say: 'Father?' That seems strange and yet sweet, because I have always thought of you somewhat as my father and master and guide. But now that to everyone else you are Father Stéphane; I love to call you by the name that now you bear for me alone—Michel! . . ."

Pressed close to his heart, in the intimacy of the night, she could not have called to him in a softer, more passionate voice. And seeing her thus absorbed in the ecstasy of her memories, the monk, enormously ill at ease, cast about for a means of wresting her from this obsession with the past. It was at that moment that the abbey clock rang out in the silence.

"The chapter, already!" he said, rising to his feet, with a feeling of relief.

Adélaide who with her eyes closed and a vague, far-off smile on her lips was seemingly asleep, straightened up quickly.

"Where are you going?" she said, holding out her arms. "Be patient. Stay with me, give me a few minutes more. . . . I want to explain to you. . . . Yes, be patient. . . . I will keep you only a few moments."

"I cannot," he said with gentle firmness. "It is time for the chapter. Understand me, Adé. I am not free."

But she would not willingly let him leave her, at

the very moment when her soul was finally about to open, when now at last, after so many futile words, she realized what she had to say to him: that she loved him better than all the world and that she could not live without him.

"Be fair with me," she begged bitterly. "For eight years I have interfered neither with your duties nor your obedience. This is the first time that I have besought you and you are turning me away. . . ."

Her lips quivered. She looked so forlorn that he took pity on her and began to reason with her as if she were a child.

"You are talking foolishly. You are not beseeching me, and I am not turning you away forever. You, too, be patient. Tomorrow I will see you again after the conventual Mass. If it is a fine day, wait for me as you used to, in the woods, under the oak. I will join you there after the office is over, and we shall have a longer time to talk. This afternoon I can only repeat to you: have confidence and be in peace. Your trouble is far from irremediable. Your heart has spoken too much within you. Your faith which has been too emotional must be built up again, like a house whose foundations were not strong enough. It must be built upon rock, must rest upon reason and will. You have wished to do that work alone and it is impossible. That is why you believed that you were lost. But now I, who know you better than you know yourself, am here to help you. My double rôle of priest and husband confers on me a double duty. Little by little you will emerge from the shadows. I should not be surprised if this very evening you did not feel that the worst of the crisis is over and that you are finding the light."

She listened with rapture to his words of assurance. Imperceptibly, she drew closer to him until she laid her head on his breast. He took her by the shoulders to support her and to hold her at a distance, and as she trembled and wilted at his touch and he saw her eyes give themselves to his, he forced her gently from him.

"Before going down to the inn," he said, "stop at the abbey church and try to pray a little while that God may enlighten both you and me."

"Michel," she murmured quickly, "I still have something to say to you. . . ."

But the cold, unmoving look in his eyes dominated her, and the avowal died on her lips.

"Tomorrow," he repeated, and he made the sign of the cross above her.

Once more there was only emptiness before her. A shadow, a vision substituted itself for Michel, occupied his place, an image less dazzling than the real being, but more indulgent. And it was to that shadow that Adélaide, moving her lips slowly, soundlessly, addressed the supplications, the reproaches, the unrestrained words of love to which the priest had refused to listen.

II. IN obedience to Michel's advice, after leaving the reception room, Adélaide went to the abbey church and remained there for a few minutes on her knees, her head in her hands. In a low voice she repeated the *Pater* and the *Ave* several times with a vain attempt at concentration. The simplest words had no meaning to her, her mind was too distracted. She no longer suffered. It did not occur to her to ask herself whether Michel had been gentle or severe with her. It was enough that he existed. For the time being she had no life of her own. He lived in her, thought in her. Freed from her individuality, she was filled with the peace and joy of another.

It was only later, when after dinner she was walking along the road, that the division took place. Very gradually the dearly beloved being whom she carried with her was torn from her heart. For a little while longer he remained merged with her more superficially, as if he were holding her in his arms and caressing her. Then again he became a distinct and separate entity. She found a new delight in this separation. By regaining the feeling of her own existence, she regained the power to analyze his love

and to relish it. After the almost unrealized ecstasy
of communion and intimacy, came the more lucid
ecstasy of contemplation.

She had seated herself on a low wall, facing a rain-
soaked field which a thin line of trees divided from
the others. Turning her back on the abbey, she had
no eyes for the darkening sky but only for the invisible companion beside her whose glance, so calm
and commanding and tender, instilled her with new
life.

Thinking back over the afternoon, she tried to
call to mind now all the joys which in her emotion
she had let slip by her. Like a traveler who at the
end of a journey tries to picture again in imagination
the countryside of which he has caught but fleeting
glimpses, she struggled to recall one by one the words
which, lost as soon as heard in course of their talk,
only now took on their true significance. The first
were:

"I am very happy, Adé. We are together again."

Then the reproach which had followed hard after
it, that reproach that was so bold, so touching, so
unjust:

*"You have acted very wrongly toward me. Death
could not have separated us more completely than
that unbending will of yours."*

And like certain words underlined on a page of
even type, a few sentences torn by emotion or ten-

derness from the monk's disciplined heart, stood out in her mind:

"The question so long unanswered has been always in my heart: where is my poor child? . . . I recognize my impulsive Adé. . . . My double rôle of priest and husband. . . ."

Isolated words which she did not yet link with those which preceded and followed them, consoling words whereby the monk made her his own once more, affirmed that she would be always his wife, his child, his Adé, the soul for which he was responsible before God. From those very simple phrases she drew a great happiness. She repeated them softly to herself time after time, trying to recall their exact intonation, the moment when they had been spoken. They were still singing within her when she went back rather late to the inn. She undressed quickly, cutting short her toilet. Everything she did, every movement, paralyzed their benevolent influence, interrupted their whispering. She was in haste to surrender herself entirely to them so that they might cradle her all night long. It was only when she was stretched out motionless in bed, in the quiet and the darkness, that she began to suffer. The magic charm of Michel's presence ceased to act upon her. The warm radiance given off by the memory of something very recent waned, and once the spell was broken Adélaide realized how far their talk had come from fulfilling the great hopes which she had had. As she thought soberly about it, Michel's reception seemed cold indeed in comparison with her own emotion. Little by little the words in which she had taken delight lost their reassuring quality. The others, to which she had paid less attention, like a poison which is drunk mixed with some delicious beverage, began to reveal their noxious strength, mounted with bitter flavor from her heart to her lips. First came back the priest's heartfelt words:

"If anything could have destroyed my peace, it would have been the thought that you did not share it. . . ."

The avowal which had seemed tender, betrayed the most complete indifference. In reality, for him, sustained by grace, Adélaide's disappearance had been only a trifling annoyance, a minute flaw in his inalterable felicity. Separated from her, knowing that she was unhappy and perhaps lost, he had been content to pray for her serenely. Her death, her possible damnation had not kept him from being at peace.

"O," she thought, "love is not like that! All the chains of joy which heaven could rivet on my soul would not keep me there if he were not with me!"

But Michel would never understand, his heart was too inaccessible now for worldly affection to touch it. Even the little tenderness which he still had for her was tinged with scorn. She remembered his condescending tone of voice when he had exclaimed:

"Feminine, too feminine, all contrasts and changes

of heart, the first temptation vanquished you." And he had said too: *"That is not the way of salvation."*

She had not tried to defend herself against that grave accusation, for it seemed to her that only lives rich in good works deserved salvation. The sensitive and the dreamers who could only love and suffer had to accept the hell which was reserved for them.

But Michel had not condemned her utterly. He had promised to help her, he had said:

"My double rôle of priest and husband confers on me a double duty."

The beginning of the sentence which a short time before had seemed rapturous to her, suddenly lost all importance. The last word struck chill into her heart. It was out of duty then that he would guide her, not out of the devotion that makes a mother bend over her sick child, a husband over his wife in danger. She almost heard him say:

"You have strayed from your way like a lost sheep." He had found nothing but ready-made phrases, infinitely vague, infinitely empty.

"Have confidence. . . . Your trouble is not ir-remediable. . . . The joy you are seeking is here before you, the joy which our Lord reserves for His elect."

She perceived how immensely cold and cruel he had been to her.

At least she knew clearly now what she wanted: never to lose him, never to leave him again. Barren as their brief talk had been, she remembered that with him she had ceased to suffer. She had a remedy of proven efficacy. A solution was obvious. She would never again be a nun or a wife, but she could be the sister of Michel, his spiritual daughter. She would settle down somewhere near-by. She would see him often. He would direct her soul. To him she would yield always. And her unhappiness would become tolerable because it would be periodically assuaged by his dear presence.

In truth, nothing else seemed to be able to have any effect upon her. The night did not calm her. No drowsiness, messenger of sleep, came to lull her body and her churning thoughts. Propped up on the pillows, she stared into the darkness and envisioned to herself the setting of the reception room. Michel was there and their conversation continued. She told him about her wishes and insisted that he should allow her to stay near him. Sometimes, to give force to the illusion which absorbed her, she spoke in a half-whisper. She listened in enchantment to herself repeating the simple words:

"Later, tomorrow. . . ."

She remembered then that Michel was not free to do as he wished, and at the realization her hopes were shattered. On his own initiative he could do nothing, even to save her. He belonged entirely to the Church, which was a thousand times more jealous than any human spouse. She saw again the gesture he had not been able to repress when she had said that she wished to live near him, and the look of pity which had come into his eyes at her illusions. He was right, his superiors would never permit him to have his wife close by him. They would not allow the shining example of that union broken for God to become a subject of gossip among the faithful. Platonic love following after physical love presented far too many risks. Father Athanase would be there to put his friend on his guard against yielding to such a plan. The Father Abbot would forbid any communication whatever between the husband and wife. With her dream endangered, Adélaide prepared to battle the authority of the Church. In the darkness she plotted out her defense, humbly presented her petition.

"Yes," she said, "I admit it, I was mistaken. I was not capable of reaching the heights to which I aspired. But dare you maintain that my sacrifice was in vain? If it was barren for me, it was profitable for another. I gave you that priest of whom you are so proud. I still have rights over him. Before vowing himself to God, he joined his life with mine by an oath so sacred that the Pope himself did not break it, but only suspended it. I have paid for his vocation with all my happiness. I do not ask that you give him back to me, since it is evidently his pleasure to remain. I merely beseech the possibility of seeing him, of belonging to him again even if he no longer belongs to me. Let me have him as a friend, as a guide. Is it such a great deal that I am asking?"

She pleaded with unknown judges, whose personalities were indistinct; with the Father Abbot, stern symbol of authority; with the monks, dark motionless silhouettes, assembled as she had often seen them in their stalls. A single familiar figure detached itself from that anonymous throng. Adélaide now saw Father Athanase before her, pure and kind, but wholly ignorant of human love, no better qualified than any of the others to understand or pity her. In vain she explained and importuned. He replied in a few words, simply and firmly. Repeatedly he proffered her the cross, but she shook her head. To escape the persistence of her vision, she flung herself out of bed, went on tiptoes to the window and opened it.

Peace reigned outside and everywhere in the world it seemed, except in her soul. No sound, save the soft, even murmur of the stream. No troubling, voluptuous scent. The autumn night, already like approaching winter, breathed forth a sober, ascetic, vigorous odor: the odor of water, the odor of cool darkness. Over the meadows which stretched before the inn, lay a thick cotton-like mist. And at the top of the hill, wrapped in the velvet of trees and thickets, the abbey stood out resplendent in the light of the full moon which shone between its two towers. The starless, cloudless sky was liquid and impalpable. The woods, the slopes, the fields, the whole dim countryside, bathed below in mist and above in the silvery radiance, lay in peace before its church. Alone, the great vessel, loaded with souls, floating on the deep waters of prayer, rode vigilantly above the sleeping world, extending its immense benediction over it. But for the woman who was suffering at that hour when all pain relaxes its grip and is lulled, the great pile took on a formidable, strangely living aspect. It was a human rival which Michel loved and preferred to her.

"I will take him from you," she cried within herself in defiance. "You have all the weight of the eternal in your favor, but he is mortal and I have the attraction of that which is mortal. He is not like those monks who have been yours since their youth. He has a past which nothing can efface. He has loved me, he will love me again."

A sob choked her. What good was this vain bravado by which she tried to deceive herself? In her heart of hearts she knew she had no more power over Michel. All the doors of the abbey could be opened in vain before that voluntary captive, without his thinking of availing himself of the liberty to join her. Besides, even reunion would not give them back to one another. The lover who had once intoxicated her with the vibrancy of his life, had given way now to the priest who saw her only as a soul among other souls. She remembered the gaze which a little while before he had fixed on her and which had seen neither her beauty nor her emotion, but had only plumbed her conscience. Her salvation was all that mattered to him. Doubtless, just as he had long been praying for her, he had long ago surrendered to God the task of consoling her. He was lying now in the cell which she would never see, which he forbade even her memory to penetrate. He was sleeping while she was calling out to him hopelessly. Her near presence troubled him no more than her absence had done yesterday. It was too late for her to wrest him from the happiness which she had given him.

She began to walk up and down her small room, from her window to her door. Her bare feet made almost no sound and each time she passed her mirror, the sight of her figure, white and ghostly in the moonlight, sent a pang of terror through her. Was that her disembodied soul that she saw? Was that herself as she would be in eternity—never resting, hounded, condemned unendingly to pursue the chimera of her broken love? To convince herself that she was still living, Adélaide touched her arms, her breast, her face wet with tears, or she gave a low moan which drowned for a moment the murmur of the stream. She regained consciousness then of her own existence. But how strange was this world about her, how unnaturally long were the hours! What was that countryside shining in the moonlight where nothing moved, where nothing had changed for so long? What was this interminable night? What sorcery hung over the universe that prevented another day from being born? How long, obsessed by these phantoms, must she listen to the same words being repeated over and over in her heart: *"if anything could have troubled my peace . . ."* and their inescapable corollary: "I can be happy without you, my joy does not depend on yours."

Nevertheless the certainty of not being loved did not reduce her to submission. She fought on savagely, no longer against the Church, or the Father Abbot, or Father Athanase, but against Michel, for it was clear to her that he was her first adversary, that he alone could defend her cause before those upon whom it depended. Everything might still be won if she could truly move him in her favor. But she was at a loss how to approach him; she no longer knew this being whose heart and whose body had ceased to answer hers. Then the same sentence, which had wounded her so, once more reassured her: "My double rôle of priest and husband confers on me a double duty." Failing love, in her misery she accepted the charity of the priest; and, imagining him before her, she fell to her knees at the foot of the bed and prayed to the darkness where she thought she saw him:

"O priest of God, you who have given your life for the souls of others, take pity on mine. For others it does not matter from whom their consolation comes, but I have need of your word alone, your help alone. It is a cold charity indeed that consists in dividing one's heart into ten thousand pieces so that each may have a tiny share. There is not too much in one heart to nourish another heart, in one life to save another life. But I ask only an infinitesimal part of yours, not selfishly but because no other will suffice. Is your God so harsh that He will not allow the weak to be carried by those who are strong? Am I to blame if I am blind and deaf and helpless, if I can see the light only through your eyes, if I can hear only your voice, if I fall when you no longer bear me up? O, your pity can save me, but only if it is equal to my grief. Do not be so tranquil, so full of certainty, do not be so happy. Do not say: 'This is not serious, this crisis will pass.' Do not judge so quickly. Take my pain upon yourself, bear my cross an instant."

If only, through a miracle, some angel parting the veils of night and sleep could show her to Michel as she was without him, she had no doubt that he would take pity on the misery at last revealed to him, would consent to watch over her life forever. A simple misunderstanding separated them. He had seen her a little while ago through the false lens of his happiness, while she herself, overwhelmed by the emotion of being with him again had all but forgotten her suffering. She must explain herself to him better. "I cannot live without you!" She had no more than that to say to him. But she had to convince him of it. "I cannot live without you!" Words, alas, that sounded so banal, that so many women had said before her. Perhaps he would not understand the seriousness of them. And yet . . . Live without him! The thought struck her like a scourge studded with iron that tears the flesh and makes the blood gush forth. Live without him! She got to her feet, swaying and panting. . . . Where would she go if this last effort failed, if Michel should send her away? Certainly she would not go out into the world again. The temptation which had come to her many times before in her hours of anguish, swept over her with such force that she cried out in pain. Yet her heart, her reason, her will, worn out with the struggle, received it almost gratefully. Only a last instinct, buried deep within her, struggled to repulse it. Before her she saw Michel's smile when she had spoken to him of her despair. He did not believe there could be any grief too great to bear. He would not realize the possibility of suicide until he saw her with a revolver at her temple or poison in her hands. She had no weapons, but she groped on her toilet table for the vial of atropine which never left her possession. Having found it, she raised it without opening it to her lips, imagining Michel was there.

"Look," she said to him, "here is death, here in my hands. It is the last friend left me, my only refuge if you send me away. This is no idle threat. I have made my choice, now you make yours. Remember, if you desert me, no law human or divine can hold me on earth, and that God in whom you believe will hold you responsible."

She set the vial back on the table. She was certain she had found the words that assured her of victory. Even if Michel's heart was untouched, his conscience would be troubled by such a tragic supplication. He would not dare put her off any longer with soft, empty words. He would feel a pity for her that would be equal to her unhappiness, he would order her to live and he would permit her to love him.

The striking of a clock interrupted her fancies and the drama she was enacting by herself. Outside, a brighter, less shimmering light was taking the place of that which the moon had shed. The world stirred slightly, suspended between sleep and waking. The sun had not yet risen. The birds were not awake. Only the clock rang out live and joyous, breaking the silence. Matins. Prayer preceded work. The monks were entering the choir to sing the praises of God. Michel ceased to be the docile phantom whom Adélaide had brought through space at her will, who had sat beside her and listened to her patiently. He was a monk once more, bound by his vows, kneeling in the stalls with his brothers. Nevertheless she was glad that he was no longer asleep. The memory of her was alive now within him. She hoped it would bring her comfort.

She had again gone over to the window and stood

looking at the abbey. The air which a short time before had been fuel to her fever, felt icy cold to her now. She shivered in her light négligé. Her suffering changed, became less piercing and heavier. The night which had tortured her, handed her over to her sister the dawn, more redoubtable still. The growing light set everywhere about her the limits of a universe in which she had no place. The doors which had been open to a thousand possibilities closed one by one. She no longer knew what she would say to Michel. It is easy to speak when no one is listening, in the exaltation of the dark. But certain words are too heart-rending to be spoken in the outside air. Daylight forces souls to be silent, grief to hide away.

A train stopped at the station, then started up again. Two servants came out of the hotel and went to the well. She could hear them talking. One of them burst into a hearty laugh. Someone came around the bend in the road. He was singing. Refreshed by sleep, everyone was joyously taking up his daily task, while Adélaide, worn out by lack of sleep, quailed at the hours before her. The too glaring light burned her like a red-hot iron. She pushed down the window, drew the shades, then lay down on the bed and closed her eyes. The light still glowed through her lids. She buried her face in the pillows. She continued to struggle with invisible enemies. The Father Abbot, Father Athanase, Michel, talked confusedly around her. A strange ceremony was beginning. She was advancing into the choir of the abbey, clothed and veiled in white. Michel was beside her. He held her hand in his. He was putting a new gold ring on her finger. Dom Athanase said aloud: "Those whom God hath joined, let no man put asunder." The Father Abbot, in miter and stole, mounted to the altar and read the marriage epistle:

"Husbands, love your wives as Christ has loved his Church. He who loves his wife loves himself, for no one has ever hated his own flesh. . . . This is a great sacrament." Adélaide's breathing became more regular. She still heard the whistling of a train, and a bird singing. . . . Then in her ear a voice repeated: "This is a great sacrament." "What sacrament is great? What does this mean?" she thought, struggling to hold on to reality. Forms, images, sounds, light, faded from her consciousness. Darkness engulfed them and closed over them. Her muscles relaxed. A quick, gentle, all-powerful hand lifted the burden which weighed upon her heart. She slept.

III.

IT is no way true that nature bestows its blessings on all alike, gives to all the same joy. No matter how bright the sun, there are shadows through which it does not pierce. It does not warm the heart weighed down with grief, the body twisted in agony.

As Adélaide climbed to the abbey that morning, she came upon a shrew-mouse lying all but dead in the road. The enemy which had met and vanquished it had fled, frightened away doubtless by someone's approach. The blood was running from its gaping side and one paw was half eaten away. She stopped to examine it, and not knowing how to help it or how to bind up that tiny, still quivering body, she covered it with fresh leaves to protect it against the flies, and hid it beside the road so that no child would torment it. Then she went on, carrying that humble sorrow in addition to her own.

Although it was still some time before she was to meet Michel, she did not go into the abbey church, feeling too tired to pray, but went straight to the bench under the oak tree where Father Athanase had so often talked to her. A few yards to her right, in the middle of the wall surrounding the monastery, was the cloister gate. No monk could come out without her seeing him. Before her lay the great green valley, encircled with hills. There were indications of approaching autumn. September was already blowing an immense cool current across the summer days. Here and there in the trees a yellowing branch, like the first white lock in a woman's hair, showed that unostentatiously, in still vigorous nature, winter and death were already working. Although the atmosphere was clear, it did not have the limpidness of mid-summer. An impalpable veil, which was neither cloud nor mist, but a certain quality of the air, lay stretched over the pale blue heavens, over the fields and the dim horizons. It softened colors and outlines and gave a delicious softness to the light.

Adélaide looked unmoved at the beauty of the day. The fatigue of her long vigil, along with her apprehension over the interview which she hoped would be decisive, weighed upon her. She found herself in a strange state, in which agitation was mixed with enervation, fever with torpor. She thought of the mangled shrew-mouse, of all those little animals who bleed and die every moment in the water and the fields and the air, and to whom God has given no voice so that, their grief unknown, they might not disturb the surface calm of nature. She thought of all the hearts torn as hers was, on whom human dignity imposes the same silence. It seemed to her she heard the fearful plaint of agony which would go up from the earth if an angel should suddenly lift, even for a second, the seal upon the world's spiritual and bodily suffering. Only a few of the fortunate are deceived by the surface splendor of things. For her, that brilliant morning was an imposture, a screen concealing universal tragedy.

It might be that her own beauty was likewise a mask concealing her grief. So this morning she had taken no pains with it. She wore her simple, woolen traveling dress. Her hair was not waved, and the too regular manner in which she had arranged it made her look old. No rouge gave life to her complexion rendered sallow by sleeplessness. But none the less her pain found no true reflection in her face. Sickness and poverty readily provoke pity because they are revealed by sunken eyes and wasted bodies. But love driven to desperation manifests itself only by tears, the common sign of all grief, the most puerile as well as the most noble, and they consequently carry no conviction. She must take care not to cry in front of Michel, for tears soften those who shed them. After they have flowed, a grateful relaxation comes when the weary spirit will listen to any promise, will grasp without discrimination at all hopes of happiness. She must control herself, and perhaps be silent at first. Silence is eloquent. Yet it presented disadvantages. If she were silent, Michel would take the initiative. She knew that she was too easily led by his voice, too quick to believe him. He would convince her perhaps that it was best for her to reënter the cloister, he would win her assent, then he would send her away forever. The great danger was that she would let herself be lulled, enraptured as she had been the day before by his presence. In front of her husband she must be the same groping, tormented soul that she was away from him. She must beware of him, not look at him, scarcely listen to him. She would have to talk, but not lyrically as she had done in the night, for an impassioned outburst would have no effect on his happiness, would bring only condescension and scorn.

The clock had rung out the appointed hour. Michel was late. Adélaide felt no resentment as yet. The delay gave her an opportunity to plan out her course of action so that nothing should be left to chance in this interview which she believed would either save or condemn her. But lack of sleep dulled her mind. At moments, her eyes closed. She stretched out her arm on the back of the bench, and leaned her head with its churning thoughts upon it. Then she caught herself up and began to marshal her attack step by step. She would have to point out, simply, the error of the past, the futility of a sacrifice of which God was not the object, the disaster to which it led, the unshakeable supremacy of human love in her heart, and the certainty that she could no longer live away from Michel. When she had finished, she would take the vial of atropine from her bag. Rising to her feet, she would have to draw away from her husband. And she repeated the words which she had planned in the night:

"Look, Michel. Here is death, here in my hands. It is the last friend left me, my only refuge if you send me away. . . . I have made my choice, now you make yours. It is perfectly simple, perfectly clear. Either life with you or death without you. And the God in whom you believe will hold you responsible for my soul."

She was no longer so certain of victory. She realized that Michel's first concern would be to snatch the poison from her. He would succeed easily, being much stronger than she. The struggle would be short and would end with his triumph. Then, having saved her after his fashion, from death only, perhaps he would have a feeling of revulsion toward her. Perhaps he would insult her by imagining it some odious blackmail, would think it a comedy put on merely to win his sympathy. How would she be able to convince him that at the moment when she had armed herself with the poison, she had not foreseen that he would prevent her from drinking it? She fell into despair. The test to which she had looked for salvation would be a failure and the terrible conflict would continue without having been brought to any solution.

Abruptly, her meditation was interrupted. She had just seen two men emerge from the cloister gate, one of whom was dressed in monk's garb. It was Michel. She rose eagerly from the bench. Life was sweet, after all. She felt, suddenly, the warmth of the sun on her hands and on her cheeks. The songs of the birds, the blue of the sky ceased to be a taunt to her unhappiness, became something reassuring, like a father's smile. Her weariness left her. Her blood which a moment before had been sluggish, coursed through her veins like a sudden flow of sap. A dangerous illusion of newness enchanted her, banished her fears. She could do nothing against this swelling hope. And, her heart pounding, she hurried toward Michel.

Although she accused him of indifference, he too had suffered poignantly on her account and had passed a great part of the night in troubled anxiety. Though he had believed from the first moment that the very fact of her coming to him proved her saved, he realized that her return solved none of her problems. While she had been evoking his every word in the darkness, he had been recalling hers with an almost equal torment. Without fully comprehending the seriousness of her trouble, and making all allowances for her "woman's exaggeration," he perceived how difficult his task was to be and what a responsibility he must henceforth assume. Having racked his mind in vain for a course of action that would reconcile his human and his religious duties, he went, after matins, to bare his difficulties to Father Athanase, his director and friend.

The latter was preparing to leave for Namur. He had no time to examine the case thoroughly. It was too grave and it found him wholly unprepared. His first reaction was one of extreme disquietude that Adélaide was in Evolayne. Already he pictured her to himself as making a scene, reclaiming her husband, and he showed himself severe.

"Have her go away, have her go away as soon as possible," he exclaimed. "She must understand that she has no more rights to you. I cannot authorize you to receive her freely in this way."

Without revolt, but firmly, Michel pleaded his wife's cause:

"I will do whatever I am ordered," he said. "But I think it would be dangerous to send her away abruptly. She is suffering, her life is all confusion, she thinks she has lost her faith. She has not come to me to turn me from my duty, but because she has no other friend. Ought I to refuse her the spiritual aid which I would give to anyone else? It seems to me that would be a cruelty. She has lost her strength; unless someone helps her she may fall utterly from grace, and she will listen only to me."

Father Athanase threw a quick, piercing look at his friend and saw that though he was torn by Adélaide's grief, his faith was unshaken and that he was ready to obey.

"Very well," he said gently, "I shall reflect. Tomorrow I shall speak to the Father Abbot and we shall examine what shall be done. You are right, it is better not to be hasty. I have a feeling that some day your wife will reënter the convent. One does not lose faith this way after one has regained it. Besides, what place is there for her in the world, with a husband who is living and a priest? It is a trying, an impossible situation for her. If her health will not allow her to lead the life of the cloister, perhaps she might enter a less rigorous order, become a teacher or a nurse. I shall see. I shall make inquiries. Receive her again today, since you have promised her. Try to calm her, to turn her toward God. Later, I shall do what I can. I understand how her unhappy lot must preoccupy you. She is passing through a difficult period and it is hard for you. But let us hope for the best. A great trial always brings great good. Above all, my friend, do not be troubled."

That last word brought comfort to Michel. It was the imperious watchword which for eight years he had obeyed, to which, little by little, he had come to submit by second nature. Besides, the interview which he was to have with Adélaide did not possess the same definitive aspect for him that it did for her. He did not know that she was hesitating between death and life and that an ill-advised word might weigh down the balance on the dark side. He hoped to use the power which he had over her to instill some confidence in her regarding the future, but he had no thought of going further or of giving her, today, any definite advice. He deemed that time and grace, always slow to act, would calm Adélaïde's soul better than any words or poor efforts of his. While she was waiting for their meeting in silent, lonely concentration, he prepared himself for it as best he could in the midst of his accustomed duties. In the morning, he had to devote himself to several retreatants who had come to spend a few days in the abbey. One of them, whom he was directing, joined him after conventual Mass. They were coming out from the abbey gardens together when the monk saw his wife. His heart leaped toward her. However, he mastered his impatience. His young penitent was about to leave Evolayne and he wished to give him a final word of advice. In Adélaïde's case, nothing was pressing. She was free. He would have plenty of leisure—today, tomorrow, later—to see her. It was better that their conversation that morning should be brief, since he had nothing precise to say to her. While she was hurrying to meet him, he walked toward her without haste. She was coming from a long anxious wait, feverish from her bad night and the obsession of a single thought, while he, on the contrary, having been up since five o'clock, distracted by a thousand duties, arrived refreshed by work, as calm as she was ungovernable. Even before they had exchanged a word, she felt how completely they were strangers to one another. The joy which she had felt at seeing him, vanished when he nodded his head to his companion who had stayed behind, and said:

"Will you wait a little longer, Adé? I have still a few words to say to that young man. I should like to go to the station with him. Do you mind?"

She did not hide her disappointment. Her eyes filled with tears, her lips trembled. He saw that her lids were red and swollen. She had been crying, she was going to cry again. She could not bear anything, even the little delay he was asking of her. In spite of himself, he felt pity for her weakness, but he thought it best not to show it.

"Enjoy this fine sunshine a little while," he said, affecting gayety. "What a glorious day! With such a sky, and such a view, who could doubt the goodness of God! His benediction is over everything."

"Except over the shrew-mouse," she thought, "and over me, and over so many miserable beings. . . ." Through her tears, everything looked hazy and somber to her. Very low, plaintively, she murmured:

"I can no longer see."

Her tone was so pathetic that his heart went out to her. But placed between two duties, from a spirit of sacrifice he chose the less pressing, the less dear: the young stranger in place of his wife, the soul knowing no pain in place of that tormented one which he was leaving unwittingly at the gates of death. The stern ecclesiastical discipline paralyzed his impulse of tenderness. The Church makes a virtue of serenity. It repeats constantly to its priests, to the faithful: "Even when you are suffering keep the appearance of joy; when your heart is a restless sea, let your face, your voice, your gestures be tranquil and assured." Michel hid his true feelings from Adélaide. It was not apparent that he was taking seriously that distress which none the less moved him deeply.

"Come," he said, smiling. "You have eyes to see. Wipe away your tears and all the light of this beautiful day will enter into you. I will soon be back. Be in peace, my Adé."

He might have left her his very real anxiety, since it was that alone for which she thirsted. But he did not. The hungry, despairing look which she raised to him was met with one as clear, as untroubled, as cruel for her as the blue of the sky.

"Go," she said. "Take your time. I can wait."

Human resistance is immense, but a little thing can break it. A person can endure hunger and thirst for a long time, but let him drink a drop of water, eat a crumb of bread and his torment is forthwith doubled. Adélaide had borne months and years of absence, then, the afternoon before, she had found Michel only to lose him again. At the moment when she thought she was going to be able to feast herself upon his presence, a new privation was imposed on her. The waiting thus prolonged became intolerable. She went back to the bench under the oak and sat down once more. The private path, reserved for the monks, which Father Stéphane and his young companion were descending, passed beneath her. Leaning over, she could see their two figures through the trees. Michel was walking slowly, bending toward his friend. His gestures showed that he was talking animatedly. She could not make out his words, but she could hear his voice. Suddenly, she felt further away from him than she had behind the grilles of the cloister, or in her wanderings. She was being halted on the threshold of a mysterious life which she could not imagine to herself, whose interests and incidents and personages would ever be strange to her. In the heart which had belonged to her, she now occupied only the humblest place. Even at this hour for which she had yearned so long and which he was to have devoted to her, he left her for a stranger, he deliberately cut short their precious time together. Soon the monks' luncheon would interrupt them as yesterday the chapter had done. She would not have time to explain herself. And besides, all the words which she had prepared, eloquent still when she addressed them to a phantom, to a memory, to the old Michel, seemed futile to her since she had seen the new man again, the priest unshakeable in his joy. A cry of pain loses its note of anguish when it falls on a cold heart. She exaggerated to herself the insensibility, more apparent than real, of the monk. To each of her plaints he would answer with that serene look with which he had crushed her a few moments before. He would not believe in her despair. He would smile at seeing the poison in her hands. What separated them was that imperturbable peace which everywhere covered the monk's soul, an armor without a flaw through which she could reach and wound that Knight of God. Besides, even if she succeeded in moving him, what could she ask of him? She no longer felt that the little compassion and solicitude which he could offer her would be enough. Even if he permitted her to remain in Evolayne, she would see him only rarely, when he was free and had no other duties. He would always be afraid of yielding overmuch to human tenderness, he would begin to avoid her as consistently as she sought him. As long as she lived, she would be a burden and a care to him, which he would grow to detest . . . as long as she lived. . . .

With those intolerable words, temptation swept through her again. Death seemed as much a physical need as food and sleep. Once more time stopped still, each minute was a century. She longed to exchange this eternal waiting for eternal oblivion. No matter how it was considered, Michel was lost to her. They were following two different roads which would never join. She wondered whether the shrew-mouse was dead yet. Would her own disappearance have more importance for the world than the extinction of that short life? Would she leave a more lasting trace? She did not believe so. The image of her would soon grow dim in Michel's heart. He would weep for her for a time, then he would banish his vain grief. Living, he had a task to fulfill among the living, and he would find this world, from which she had departed, no less beautiful, no less divine.

Half past eleven rang out from the abbey. Time which seemed unmoving was passing, and still Michel had not come back and her opportunity was growing less and less. He would not be able to hear her out this morning any more than he had yesterday afternoon. He would bestow a few encouraging words on her and would send her away again, setting another rendezvous as uncertain as this one. But if he found her with death within her, he would not dare to leave her. To be present with the dying is a higher duty for a priest than obedience to his rule, and he would forget everything for her.

Thus she was led back always to clutch despairingly at the same thought. Her sleeplessness, and the nervous exhaustion to which her long secret struggle had reduced her, made it a fixed idea. Waiting was ceaselessly undermining the frail rampart of courage and reason which still defended her life.

It was at that moment that she heard steps and saw one of the religious approaching on her right. He did not wear the scapular of the monks. It was a lay brother, the one who received visitors and to whom she had spoken the afternoon before. He was looking about him as if he were searching for someone. Recognizing Adélaide, he came toward her.

"I beg your pardon, Madame, I thought I might

find Father Stéphane here. Someone is asking for him in the reception room."

She replied:

"He has gone to the station with a young man. He will soon be back."

Then, very low, in an almost suppliant voice, she added:

"I have been waiting for him for a long time."

But what did it matter to the brother that she was impatient or that she had a right to see him first? He bowed.

"Thank you, Madame. I shall see if I can catch sight of the father on the path. I have a letter to give him. It is urgent I am told."

Adélaide lost all hope. Her unbalanced imagination was already twisting the incident so as to draw another bitterness from it. Someone was insisting on seeing Michel, and she did not hesitate to believe that he would sacrifice her to another stranger. The thought was beyond all endurance. She could not have the interview put off until tomorrow. Her lot must be decided this morning or never. She did not have enough strength to carry her through another night, and if the only way she could hold Michel was by death . . .

But death intimidates even those whom it fascinates. To the fearful unknown, the familiar grief still seemed preferable. Before a person reaches the point where he will destroy his own existence, some uncontrollable paroxysm of love, or some thought-obsession, or some force of present circumstances must blind him to what he is doing, must prevent his imagining that eternity into which he is about to cast himself. Suicide is rarely a reasoned act, but rather a desperate gesture which leaves chances of life. It was thus that Adélaide suddenly envisioned it. Who knows, perhaps the vial which she had in her bag contained a poison that was too weak or too strong. In risking death, perhaps she would escape it. If Michel could only know that she was capable of killing herself for him, if he could see her stricken, having consumed the poison, he would know that to save her he would have to save both body and soul. He would never dare forsake her again. The danger she ran would in the end give them back to each other. That single chance shrouded the peril from her.

While she was lost in those thoughts, Michel was coming quickly up the path. He had stayed longer at the station than he had intended, for the train had been late. He felt guilty about Adélaide. He sensed how heartless this long wait must appear to her. He hastened so as not to cut any shorter the half hour which he could still devote to her. At the top of the path, opposite the cloister gate, the abbey porter stopped him and handed him the letter. He glanced through it rapidly, and though it was important, it in no way changed his plans. He scribbled a reply on the back of the envelope, making an appointment for the afternoon. Then he walked a few steps with the lay brother, begging him to keep away all visitors that morning. Adélaide, following their colloquy from a distance, interpreted it in her own way. He was certainly going to put her off in favor of this other stranger who was seeking him. "I will come," he was saying, "right away, just as soon as I can dismiss that woman who is waiting for me over there." A last desperate wave of revolt swept over her, clouding her reason. Threatened by being abandoned again she ceased to fear death, and having but one means whereby she could hold Michel, she used it. Opening her bag, she turned her back so that from the distance he should not see her lift something to her lips. She had to gulp at it several times, for the liquid was bitter. Nevertheless she had time to empty the vial before Michel, having dismissed the brother, walked toward her free, his heart full of tenderness, not knowing that he was too late.

IV

. SHE heard and recognized the steps that were approaching, but she did not turn her head. It was no longer Michel that she was waiting for, but a visitor from whom her flesh shrank, one whom she had imprudently summoned and who would not tarry long in coming. The bitter philter which she had just drunk made her a new being, indifferent to that which an instant before had obsessed her. All the torments of her love and abandonment seemed as nothing compared with that destitution into which she was entering. Everything which had been her life was already fading from her. There was only a future of a few hours before her, and then that terrible beyond which would claim her soul. What good now was Michel's presence at her side, what good were his pity and his tenderness? He could no longer prevent her from being alone.

She was still seated on the bench, her body bent forward a little, her eyes closed, the taste of the poison still in her mouth. She hid the empty vial in her closed hands. As Michel approached, he noticed that she was trembling—from anger, doubtless. He guessed how indignant it had made her to see him devoting to someone else the time which he should have given to her. He was consequently not at all astonished to find her silent and hostile.

"Forgive me, Adé," he said gently. "In our ministry we cannot always dispose of our time at will. A thousand unforeseen duties call us."

What was this vain murmur she was hearing as she listened to the waters of death seething and rising within her? Already her soul, half engulfed, was struggling despairingly.

"I am free to be with you at last," Michel went on. "Since yesterday I have thought of you constantly. I want to make you as certain as I am myself that your doubts will soon be dispelled. You have only to pray."

She was silent. If she had dared pray at that moment, she would have implored only that her life might be spared, but, having sinned, she could not ask a miracle. The hope which had lured her on, which had given her the strength to carry out her irreparable act, had vanished. She no longer doubted that she had drunk a fatal draught. In a little while she would feel the poison gnawing at her. Then her faculties would fail her, she would lose consciousness; then the death agony, the coffin, the tomb. Fear, striking through her, made her open her eyes. How far away, how beyond her reach, the nearest tree suddenly seemed! She would not have dared to touch its green leaves, to place her hand against its bark.

She no longer had those rights which life gives over things around her. She was no longer part of the universe. She was outside it, excluded from it. The countryside fell away before her eyes as if glimpsed in flight. Death was already laying hold on her, drawing her out of this world in which she had lived. The things and being which she had abandoned, were abandoning her. Meanwhile Michel was speaking.

"I have just witnessed a prodigious example of how grace may return to one whom it seems to have deserted," he said. "It has greatly comforted me in my anxiety about you. The young man whom you saw with me a few minutes ago is one of my penitents who for a long time seemed hopelessly lost, led astray by the violence of his own passion. He even denied God. Fortunately he still kept up his contact with me and I was able to persuade him to come and make a retreat among us. The result was startling. He left here utterly changed, so strengthened in his faith that now the religious life alone holds any attraction for him, and I am certain that after a time of trial, he will come back and enter the abbey permanently. If only I may soon hear words from you, Adé, similar to those which he spoke in leaving me. God often uses his humblest priests to work the most remarkable transformations. It is the inexpressible sweetness of our difficult task."

She straightened up and looked at him with sudden hatred. He was alive, everything about him was alive: his body, his soul; his body in the fullness of health, his soul in the fullness of strength and certainty. She felt a horror for his unshakeable peace, and she longed to tear it from him. She was tired of suffering alone; she wanted to see him struggling in the darkness with her. In a low, vibrant voice, half sarcastic, half reproachful, she asked:

"How many souls have you saved?"

He answered humbly:

"None. We are but instruments. It is God alone who acts."

She persisted, with still greater bitterness:

"How many souls saved will you offer to your Master in exchange for the one which you have lost?"

He paled at her glance.

"What soul have I lost?"

"Mine."

"That would indeed be a matter of eternal remorse for me, but I know you well. I know that your happiness was not in me, that I could never have been sufficient to you."

She turned her head a little and he could see only her trembling mouth.

"Yet, Michel, I am dying because you forsook me."

Something warned the monk that her words were no figure of speech, but the truth itself. He felt it ring out in his heart. Yet in his resolution not to let himself be troubled, he replied with a gentleness that was a little insipid, almost puerile:

"One says that, and yet one lives on."

"Do not jest."

Her voice no longer expressed anger, only a sort of tranquil, irresistible authority. At the same time, she opened her closed hands. She handed him the empty, open vial. Without understanding, he took it and turned it over. On the red label he saw the name of the poison. And at the sight, he cried out in such horror that his voice reverberated among the trees:

"Adé, Adé, what have you done?"

"What those do who are in despair."

There at last she had her triumph! She had torn his happiness from him, so violently, with such cruelty, that that strong man seemed suddenly the weakest of the weak and the blood from the torture of his soul filled his eyes as tears.

Grief spares no one upon the earth. Its apparent injustice hides a profound impartiality. Only its methods are different. The favorites whom for years it seems to take delight in torturing are no more cruelly treated in the end than those whom it feigns to neglect. For the latter will some day be swept up in its grasp with a relentless fury. Everything which Adélaide had suffered through ten years, Michel suffered in turn within a few minutes. On the calvary to which she had climbed step by step, he joined her, reached, as she had reached, absolute destitution and that despair in which he had not believed. The transformation to unhappiness was made in one quick

271

conflagration. He ceased to feel the divine benediction upon him, to be part of a world where nothing was irreparable, where every sorrow had its consolation. Faced by irremediable disaster, he looked with anguish at the wife whom he had left only with the conviction that he would be reunited with her in another world, and whom now he was losing in a double death. He felt no aversion for her because she was damned; he loved her, he loved her. He went down with her into the depths of darkness, into the stygian blackness of her crime. But neither faith nor hope of salvation could abandon the heart of him who was a priest. Even in his turmoil, a last ray of reason reminded him that his most pressing duty was toward her who had no other intercessor save himself. To cure the soul so deeply affected, the life of the body must first of all be preserved. The monk stood up hurriedly and forced her to her feet.

"Come," he said, drawing her after him, "come with me."

"Where?"

"To the abbey!"

She held back rebelliously.

"Please, my dear one," he begged her. "Time is passing. You must be taken care of immediately. Don't you want to come with me? Very well, then, I will telephone to the city and be back in a moment."

But she seemed rooted to the ground and she held on to him with all her strength.

"No," she groaned. "If we go to the abbey, we won't be alone, they will still try to separate us. If you leave me even for a moment, how can I be sure of seeing you again? Now you are thinking only of saving me, of seeking remedies, but in a little while when some one of your penitents, or anyone at all, asks for you in the reception room, you will never think of me again."

Her pathetic, absurd words brought tears to his eyes once more, for it proved to him how cruel he had been toward her. He must have made her suffer indeed, if she believed him capable of abandoning her at such a moment, of forgetting her peril at the sight of the first-comer.

"Don't ever go away from me again," she implored. "That little word means only a very short time now. Stay with me, let me lean upon you. It will not be a long trial for you and then you will be free forever. O, Michel, I have lived so long alone, I don't want to die without you."

She clung to him, her arms clasped about his neck, and he did not force her away. He no longer feared that lovely body which had ceased to be an instrument of temptation. It was already undermined by death, its beauty, though still intact, was menaced, was witness to the inevitable victory of dust over flesh, and of the vanity of the appearances which human love holds dear. He pressed her trembling form to him as if to shield it from harm and to communicate his own life to it. Motionless, her eyes closed, Adélaide forgot everything in the sweetness of that embrace.

Michel, however, did not lose sight of the danger from which she must be saved.

"I shall not leave you, Adé, I promise you. I shall do whatever you wish, my dear one. But let me care for you; we cannot remain here."

She opened her eyes. Things about her appeared in a dazzling of light, then seemed to vanish in their own brightness. She had the impression that space was becoming larger, was creating an immense hollow about her. Dizziness overwhelmed her and she longed to be within the protecting walls of a room. She looked uncertainly, terrifiedly, at Michel.

"Yes," she stammered. "Let us go. Take me to the inn."

He yielded. The abbey was nearer, but help could also be gotten at the inn. He walked beside her, supporting her, and they took the path leading down to the station. Under the trees the way was so narrow that she wanted to walk alone. Then her eyes clouded again, she staggered, and he caught her just as she was about to fall. After that, he kept his arm tight about her, and she let herself be led, docilely, unresistingly, her face hidden in his shoulder.

V. HE had forced himself to think of everything, to foresee everything. Although a monk, he still practiced medicine in the abbey and, in urgent cases, near-by. He had written a prescription, had sent a bicyclist to Dinant for certain drugs, had telephoned to two doctors. Then, knowing that at the bedside of his wife, as soon as she began to suffer, he would be only a distracted man, incapable of worthily fulfilling his rôle of priest, he sent word to Father Athanase, forgetting that the latter that very morning had set out after matins to officiate at a marriage in Namur.

With these arrangements made, Michel could only wait. He forced himself to keep up his hopes so that his confidence, real or feigned, might be a comfort to Adélaide. He would have liked to cradle her in his arms, to console her with the tenderest of words, but although they were alone now in the room where she had so yearned to see him, she paid no attention to him. Her eyes, to which the abnormal dilation of the pupils lent an unbelievable brightness, appeared to flash a sort of fierce defiance whenever they met his, then turned quickly away. She wandered ceaselessly around the small chamber, picking up little objects and setting them down again. She had put on a flowing white négligé, trimmed with lace, and at one moment she shiveringly wrapped a woolen scarf about her neck, at another took it off again. Tormented by thirst, she drank a little of the hot drink which Michel had had prepared for her. The too sweet beverage sickened her and for some minutes a violent nausea held her to her bed. A little later, she went over to her dressing table to arrange her hair. Her face was indistinct in the mirror. She wiped the clear glass several times, then pressed her fingers to her eyes and seemed astonished not to find them wet.

"I ought to be crying," she remarked. "Yes, I ought to cry to have found so little love here on earth."

But she understood what was interfering with her sight, and as Michel was standing close beside her, following with anguish the first symptoms of her poisoning, she asked him without looking at him, in a tone of desperate nonchalance:

"Well, doctor, what do you say? Am I going to suffer much? Shall I soon have done with this world?"

He put his two hands on her shoulders so that she might feel his reassuring presence.

"Do not talk that way, my dear one. There is nothing to be afraid of. My colleagues will soon be here and we shall save you. I am certain of it."

"Ah," she said between closed teeth, "it makes little difference. I have no desire to live."

Bending over her, he begged her:

"Not even for me, Adé?"

Without answering, she pushed him away abruptly, and dropping into an armchair by the window, gazed out at the shadowless countryside bathed in the noonday sun.

"To leave that," she murmured as if talking to herself, "it's not easy to leave that. Little wonder that we fear the cold and the darkness of death. If I were a tree, or a blade of grass, or an animal, I would wish to live, but to be a woman. . . . To hope and wait, always, always in vain, day after day, night after night. No. I can bear it no longer. For what can I do, where can I go? O, you say to live for you! . . ."

She interrupted herself and half turning toward Michel, gave a quick, ironic laugh.

"Live for you!" she repeated. "For a long time that was my only purpose in life, but I saw that marriage seemed a chain to you so I broke it, and now I am freeing you completely by dying. From the moment you ceased to find your happiness in me, your pity was not enough."

Not only because he was trying to say the words she was yearning to hear, but because he believed he could not live on if he did not save her life and her soul, he answered:

"My happiness is in you."

"That is not true," she cried fiercely. "No, it is not true, for I belonged to you as completely as any ob-

ject could, and you renounced me joyously. Many
people admired you then, many people praised your
sacrifice, and yet don't you think . . ."

She buried her head in the monk's shoulder and
finished with a sob:

"Don't you think it would have been better if you
had just loved me?"

Very low, because he was crying too, he murmured:

"Yes, Adé."

For everything was now clear to him and it no
longer had to be explained how dearly she had paid
for his vocation.

"Love you," he said softly, his lips against her
cheek so that each word he spoke formed a kiss, "yes,
I should have loved you better, I should have protected you against yourself, I should have refused
your sacrifice, your so unjustifiable sacrifice since you
were making it only for me. I did not understand.
Who understands anything here on earth until it is
too late? Forgive me. . . ."

She drew back, slipping from his arms, and she
moved her lovely head to and fro on the back of the
chair.

"No," she said, "it is really too easy, just to say
'forgive me,' and have everything wiped out. Why
should I have pity on you, Michel? Did you ever have
pity on me? You accepted my sacrifice simply and
joyously, without stopping to think that it was be-

yond my strength. You did not spare me, you forced me to go higher and higher up that cruel road which broke my body and my soul. Sometimes, I besought you and wept before you, but you were unmoving. You thought that it was good for me to suffer. See, now, where it has brought me. You are convinced that suffering is holy and necessary, but have you ever the right to bless it when it is someone else it tortures? Salutary as it may seem to you, how do you know that it is not more than that other person can bear? O, you were cruel, cruel! Take my heart within yourself, take my love, you who have never loved, and try to be in peace now with that burning, devouring fire in your breast."

He listened trembling to her heart's cry, with no thought of interrupting it. To be with her now was a just expiation. Her words, pronounced already from outside the world, scarred him forever, but he did not find them too severe. He endorsed them and amplified them, sparing himself nothing.

He remembered the day in the woods when Adélaide had clung to him, her face pale, and how she had avowed her weakness when she groaned:

"It is too much, it's too great a sacrifice."

Yet, untroubled, he had urged her on. Because he had found in his own suffering a richer life, he had never considered that she might be crushed by hers. Only now did he understand the infinite diversity of human nature, the disastrous weakness of human hearts, the relentlessness of passion. Now at last he denounced himself for his blindness.

But not even the excitation of the poison could change Adélaide's character or make her implacable. Already she had given vent to all the bitterness and anger within her. Looking at the monk's distraught face, she was horrified at her heartlessness and she flung her arms about his neck.

"I feel no hatred toward you, Michel. O, never think that I do. I did not mean to make it so hard for you. It is the fever of life which still makes me say such foolish things, but it will soon be past, and remember that I have long ago forgiven you everything. You have nothing to reproach yourself for; I alone am responsible for my destruction. You had no way of understanding what I was trying to do for you, you could not foresee that nothing would console me. There is no man or woman who does not forget; time heals every wound. A love such as mine is a rare thing. And see how useless it was, what calamity it has brought. In seeking only you, in thinking only of our happiness together, how can I have lost you so completely? For I have lost you, Michel, in this world and the next."

The monk shuddered imperceptibly. Not for an instant since he had entered the room with Adélaide had he ceased to think of both her temporal and her spiritual salvation. He could not understand why the doctors whom he had summoned, and the messenger who had gone to Dinant, had not yet arrived. In anguish, he contemplated the passing time and his own helplessness. He feared equally for the body which was in danger and for the soul which was beset by sin. But for the instant the soul seemed to be waking. Caught still in the web of its crime, it was stirring fitfully, giving a little flutter to its wings. Perhaps now he might be able to exert some influence over it, bring it back to the life of grace. Slowly, enunciating each word carefully so that she could not fail to understand them and his meaning, he spoke:

"Death—whether it comes soon or later—even death, Adé, will separate us only if you wish it. All the creatures of God must meet in God."

He waited a few moments. She did not reply. Her lips moved, not to speak but with the slow, painful movement of thirst. He rose and brought water to her, then he knelt beside her again and drew her to him, gently tilting back her head so that he might read any thoughts which were reflected in her face.

"God," he repeated insistently, certain that in offering her that single name he was offering her the supreme assistance.

But through the dark, immensely dilated pupils which he was watching so intently, the soul, sinking back once more, gave no sign. Twice Adélaide shook her head in refusal.

"The God I dreamed of," she breathed, "was a God of pity . . . not this God Moloch, who thirsts for the blood of his creatures . . . this God who has demanded every sacrifice of me."

"Do not let yourself be confused," the monk protested humbly. "It is I who demanded every sacrifice of you, it is I who, because of my desire, too subtle for your love, drove you from the way of life in which God would have left you. It is I alone who prevented His grace from descending upon you. Alas, Christ will be betrayed eternally by those who believe that they are his apostles! He took upon Himself the whole cross, and I, faithless disciple, thought only of burdening your weak shoulders with it. But, Adé, it is not possible that this God whose image I have dishonored, is not yours also. You know well that He is love."

She raised herself a little, stretched out her arms with a shadowy smile, then her head dropped back wearily on her husband's shoulder. He had to lean down to catch the words which came haltingly, very low, from her lips.

"It is too late. . . . My crime is inexpiable."

"My beloved, my poor Adé," he said, struggling to communicate his own faith to her, "there is no sin here on earth which true repentance will not efface. I am a blind imperfect man, but I am a priest and I have the power to absolve every soul that weeps for its faults. As I forgive you in my name for the suffering which comes to me today through you, I can forgive you in Christ's name and reconcile you with your Creator who is infinitely more tender than I."

"I understand," she said. "You want to hear my confession. But I am afraid that would be only a fresh sacrilege. In my eyes you would again be my God."

Timidly, almost apologetically, he said:

"I have sent for Father Athanase."

She took his hand and kissed it in a wave of utter submission.

"I will do anything that you wish," she said softly. "If you want me to make my confession to you or to anyone else, I am ready. But what value will there be in an act which is done only to please you? O, Michel, you have been my whole life, the only aim of my life, and if human love is condemned, there can be no salvation for me. I shall go to eternity empty-handed, rich only in it."

She was silent and a few moments passed. The monk felt the warmth of her cheek against his. She leaned more heavily against his shoulder. He had no need to look at her to read within her. She was broken, incapable of any effort. He could find no words which might bring back life to her exhausted soul. This woman whom he loved above all others was the only one for whom he could not fulfill his rôle of priest, because in her heart he usurped the place of the Master. She understood his distress, but she could do nothing that might make it less.

"So farewell," she murmured in a low, rasping, strangely inhuman voice. "I shall not rest in peace for I know that we shall never be together again. I am dying with your name in my heart. Cover my body with benedictions and holy oil as you will, my soul will escape you even as it belongs to you. You must forget me, Michel."

He made a gesture of denial more eloquent than any words, so visibly did his whole being enter into it. By her transgression she had bound him to her more profoundly than all her acts of obedience and faith had done. Henceforth, though their double grief would be forever sterile, he would never cease to suffer through her. They looked at each other torn in heart, he because of God, she because of him. They wept, seeing the irreparable injury they had done to one another. For the last time she covered the monk's face with kisses.

"Forget me," she begged. "I am willing, I want you to. Go, be happy in heaven, and leave me to eternal darkness. There is no salvation for me. Even if I were blessed and forgiven, I would not rest in peace because I would never be able to be one with you, and become you. For eternity I would be conscious of this division, this separateness from each other which is killing me, this torment of being myself and not you."

He knew that this was no raving of delirium. It was simply that the exaltation caused by the poison was breaking down the barriers of reason and was liberating the brutal truth. It was out of the most secret depths of her life that the declaration of this monstrous desire arose, a desire divorced from any aspect of reality, a thousand times more sinful than any carnal impulse. Before this poor, forever deluded creature, who even at the gates of death turned to him, cried out to him, and still mistook him for the supreme in life, the monk, object of her idolatrous error, began to tremble. He had the impression that he was falling dizzily, that she was dragging him with her into an abyss. He resisted and prayed, but the feeling would not down that all the glorious efficacy of grace must go for nought in the bottomless pit of a misery such as hers.

It was at that moment that a car stopped outside the inn and Michel, pulling back the curtain, saw one of the doctors whom he had summoned step from it. The human aid which was arriving at last, brought him some comfort. The terrible spiritual drama in which he was taking part was interrupted. Once more he felt about him the reassuring limits of life. Pressing, necessary duties imposed themselves: to take care of Adélaide, to save her from death. Then everything would be won. With time he would be able to cure her of her love for him. He started to meet the doctor, but he had taken only a few steps toward the door when Adélaide rose to her feet, clutching wildly at the air and crying after him.

"Michel, don't go yet, don't forget me so quickly. Can't you stay even a few hours with me, is my death so long in coming?"

In a trice he was beside her. Her eyes were like a restless sea in which one could see the waves of fear running surge after surge. As soon as he spoke, she became a little calmer, and gropingly, like a blind person, she reached to touch his face.

"I can't see any more," she groaned. "Everything is black. But it is you, I can recognize you. O, even if I were a stone or an insect buried in the ground, I think I would recognize your step. Take me in your arms, put your arms around me, like this, like this. Tell me that you love me, caress me!"

He obeyed, pressing her to him. But as he did so he felt the irresistible power of death forcing them apart.

VI.

AT half past six the last train of the day stopped at the station in Evolayne. Father Athanase stepped off. With a look he took possession once more of the familiar countryside still visible in the growing twilight. The railroad track, the road, the white walls of the station and the inn stood out clearly against the dark masses of the woods and hills. The lower part of the abbey was in blackness but its towers bathed in a limpid sky where the last rays of the sun were giving way to the twinkling of a single star. The monk smiled almost amorously. No matter how short his absence, he could never come back and look without emotion at the refuge which for thirty years had sheltered his life. The memory of the young couple whom that morning he had given to each other also warmed his heart. Their home would be a Christian home. Children would be born, some of whom, perhaps, God might choose for His servitors. The thought gave him added joy. With happy step he crossed the wide meadow behind the station and plunged into the dark lower woods. The sudden coolness of the air was like a dash of water against his face. In the darkness, habit guided him up the well-known path. He walked quickly, blessing the sleep which was falling over the earth and its creatures and which gave them back each night to God. To him happiness was everywhere because his heart was in peace.

As he entered the abbey, the porter stopped him and handed him a letter which had been brought that morning in his absence and which was said to be particularly important. After a long day passed in the midst of men, the monk would have liked to find relaxation before dinner in a half hour of prayer, but he had grown accustomed to being unable to heed his own desires. No matter who the person who made claim upon him, he was ready to serve with prompt charity.

Without any irritation, without curiosity, without haste but without delay, he opened the letter and read the short note which Michel had written.

Never, in the twenty years that he had known Father Athanase, had the brother, standing indifferently near-by, seen such distress show upon his face. The muscles stood out. His ruddy complexion took on a clay-like pallor. His eyes stared in questioning and fear. Sensing, however, that he was being watched, the monk forced himself to resume an appearance of calm.

"Dear brother," he said in a voice that was almost natural, "will you take a message to the abbot? I am called to the bedside of a dying woman. It is possible I may not be back this evening."

He went out quickly. The serenity of the evening closed about him. Hidden by it, he paused a moment to gain control over himself. A passionate prayer rose from his heart for that sinful soul which he would gladly have redeemed at the cost of his own life. Was she still of this world? Might he still have time to reach her and aid her to repentance? There was no way of knowing. The letter which he held in his hand had been brought at noon. Sometimes a few hours were enough to destroy a life which at another time might fight off death interminably. He began to run in the darkness, going down the winding road which was longer but easier than the path through the woods. Ten minutes later he was in front of the inn. It was only dimly lighted, for at that time of year travelers and pilgrims rarely stopped after sunset. The innkeeper and his wife and a young servant were standing before the door with the hostile, anxious look upon their faces of those whom a tragic occurrence has wrenched from the even tenor of their ways. The monk spoke Adélaide's name.

"O, you are coming to see that poor lady," exclaimed the man, trying to bury his ill-humor under a forced note of pity. "The doctors have just left. It seems she's bad, very bad. They ought to have taken her to a hospital in the city straight off. How can they take care of her here? . . . There's no sense in it. . . . We have done all we can but Father Stéph-ane won't have anyone around."

Dom Athanase climbed the stairs. On the second floor, the sound of voices and groaning led him to a door on which he knocked without response. He opened it cautiously.

The strong, cold odor of ether was his first sensation. In the dimness, it created an atmosphere appropriate to illness. An electric light around which a silk scarf had been wrapped was casting a feeble radiance about the room. Everything was upset by the struggle which for hours three men had been making against death. In order to be able to move freely in the narrow space, they had piled the furniture one piece on top of another. Some of it was overturned. Hasty hands had plunged into drawers and closets which stood gaping open. Women's clothing, sheets, and towels were strewn here and there. On the toilet table stood a doctor's bag, an alcohol burner, bottles and tubes and medicines. The bed was partially hidden by Michel's tall, somber figure. He was bent over a white form which was stirring in his arms. At the sound of the door opening, he turned his head and recognized Father Athanase. He stopped him with a sign.

"Not now," he said very low. "Don't come in for a moment, you will frighten her."

The illness had taken the form of fear. To Adé-laide everything about her now was a threat, a danger. The contours of real objects were lost in indeterminate zones of light and shadow. Her imagination peopled the void with hideous figures. Shuddering close against Michel, she pointed them out in terror. Her delirium was all the more agonizing in that she could not speak. In vain she struggled to make herself understood, but her shrunken larynx gave forth only a series of clipped, rasping sounds which fell short of words. Finally with a supreme effort, she pronounced distinctly, imploringly, the word "day." Michel switched on the ceiling light. She thought then that she was in the midst of flames and she screamed out. He turned it off quickly. To reach the switch, he had had to leave her side. The black moving figure, ceasing to be familiar to her, now became a danger. The man she loved was no longer her defender but her enemy. With nothing to which she could turn for protection, she watched him defiantly. She was shivering with fear and when he tried to touch her, she recoiled to the other side of the bed. He stretched out his arms in an effort to calm her, but he only increased her terror. She threw herself from beneath the covers, touched the floor, fell on one knee, and rising ran to the window and tried to open it. Michel had already caught up to her. He put his arms about her, bending before the furious writhings of that body to which delirium and terror lent an abnormal strength. There was a short struggle. Then the crisis was over. Michel carried her limp form back to the bed and worked over her to restore her to consciousness. At the same time, in a low voice, he answered the questions of Father Athanase who had approached.

"It's the fifth attack. . . . Morphine injections only aggravated the condition. . . . We have tried everything . . ."

He did not finish. Strength failed him to comment further or to put his grief into words. His attitude said sufficiently clearly that Adélaide was lost. One could sense that everything he was doing was only in the hope, not of saving her, but of giving her relief. His face had grown old and was set with grim determination, a determination to endure everything to the end and to leave nothing undone in these attentions which were his last duty. Leaning over the bed, he looked fixedly at that flesh which was being destroyed, at that face which was already unrecognizable, at that heart which he had broken. Through the veil of the body he was doubtless trying to distinguish the dying flame of the soul. Father Athanase asked:

"Were you able to hear her confession?"

He shook his head, repeating Adélaide's words:

"She said, 'What is the use, in my eyes you would be God.'"

He broke down, and, his voice trembling, he explained:

"She sacrificed herself for me. . . . She entered

the cloister without a vocation . . . in order that I might pursue mine . . . she says that she has never worshiped . . . never worshiped anyone but me."

Father Athanase made a gesture of consternation. Although Michel no longer held any hope, either as a doctor or a priest, he begged:

"Perhaps you may be able to show her the truth better than I. Speak to her. There are moments when she is lucid."

One of those moments had come. The stupor which had followed Adélaide's delirium was dissipating. Her eyes were opening once more, and for the instant they no longer showed the haggard brilliance of hallucination. The intensity of her glance was abnormal, but it was human. Her eyes focused on real objects, burned into them in astonishment, doubted them. Looking at the two men standing at her bedside, she distinguished them one from the other, struggled to place them in the domain of her memory. Knowing that her sense of hearing was not affected as was that of her sight, Michel repeated loudly:

"Father Athanase is here, Adé. Do you hear? Father Athanase."

She nodded her head in assent. Michel dropped back, making way for his friend at the head of the bed. The latter bent down. His face was gentle. His lips brushed Adélaide's brow. Neither the stain of sin upon her, nor her lack of resignation to her grief, deterred his perfect charity. He spoke to her and she recognized him, for she held his hand long in hers. A few indistinct sounds escaped her mouth but she could not succeed in pronouncing a word. Her hand again pressed that of the monk, then withdrew. She seemed at the same time to be thanking him and dismissing him, too exhausted to accept any aid.

Father Athanase hesitated. He found himself confronted by something which went far beyond the limits of the immediate situation and called into question the most troubling problems. This soul had loved deeply and had suffered nobly, and yet it was lying vanquished, without hope, on the point of death. If one single time, human pain failed of its mission, and instead of saving, lost, things were not as simple upon earth as he had thought. The priest dared neither condemn nor pass judgment nor intervene in any way save by prayer in the drama which was reaching its climax before his eyes. Not knowing how to reach the erring soul which he had never understood, he turned to God. Falling to his knees, he prayed earnestly, then, rising, he bent once more over Adélaide and repeated his words several times so that she might be certain to understand.

"I shall not ask you any questions," he said. "When a soul has suffered beyond a certain point, it can be touched only by Him whose feet and hands were pierced. It seems to me that Jesus wishes to be alone with you. Put yourself in His hands, weep for your sins and implore Him, your Savior. Tell Him that you wish to love Him . . . Him alone, not His creature . . . to love Him at last."

At the same time he proffered a crucifix to the dying woman and laid it gently first on her brow, then on her mouth, then on her breast. She was conscious of its touch and sat up shivering, like a person who recognizes the approach of one whom she both loves and fears, or who hears herself called by name. She was panting a little and she seemed to be listening; there was the suggestion of a smile on her lips, timid, and suppliant, and bitter. Gropingly, she sought the cross and grasped it, then raised it high above her head as a drowning man raises above the waves the last treasure which he possesses and which he wishes to save. Her eyes riveted themselves on Father Athanase, who, after blessing her, stood upright and in a firm loud voice pronounced the formula of absolution. Two tears ran down her cheeks. She tried to speak once more, to formulate her last thought, her repentance perhaps, but she struggled in vain. Avidly as Michel listened to hear her final confidence, priceless to him, he could seize nothing. Almost immediately after, that human communication which consists of words and looks and signs came to an end. The death agony began. Her eyes rolled up. Her face became rigid and expressionless. Her movements which had been jerky and uncertain became convulsive. On the bed was only a blind form, torn this way and that by hidden forces, racked by incredible suffering, struggling confusedly to burst the bonds of life and find escape in death.

On the threshold of eternity the wait was long. The inn was absolutely still; either the proprietors had sought refuge in some other building, or they were now asleep. Adélaide's slow, hoarse breathing alone rose above the silence. The shaded light shone feebly on her white face, stained with red blemishes. Wisps of hair clung damply to her temples. All the radiant beauty which that morning had still been shining in her face was withered now.

It is not true, as it is sometimes said, that death horrifies the living. It is the supreme seduction. Never in the fullness of her youth had Adélaide been more beloved than in this hour of her fading. Not for an instant did the two priests relax the devotion with which they were watching over her. If she had only had some wish, no matter how stifled her call, they would have instantly understood and fulfilled it. But she asked nothing. They had to turn to their imaginations and invent attentions which might still be grateful to her. At regular intervals they poured a little water between her dry lips, wiped the perspiration from her forehead. Michel held her icy hand so that in her abandonment she might still have the feeling of a loving presence. Occasionally he pressed his cheek against her mouth. And for a long time, through her tortured flesh, she was conscious of the touch and replied to it with a quiver. Then that last reflex ceased. She gave no further sign of consciousness. Life ebbed within her; her pulse no longer beat. Her hands still moved feebly. She no longer swallowed the water which they gave her and it ran down her cheek in a thin, cold trickle. Seeing that he could do no more for her, Michel no longer made even a pretense of courage. He lay half sprawled upon the bed, trying to die with her, his head on her shoulder, his hand over her heart to catch its last fluttering. Watching those two forms, Father Athanase felt them endangered equally, and he tried to separate them, to recall the one who was to live to the duties of life. Leaning close to him, he said very low:

"Let us say together the prayers for the dying. It is the only help of which she now has need."

Michel raised dull eyes to his friend and with a gentle sign of refusal which brooked no contradiction, astounded him with these words:

"I am no longer a priest, no longer even a Christian!"

The scene which was being enacted there was analogous to that which Milton imagined as having lost the human race. Adam did not eat the fruit of death out of weakness or in error, but with full consciousness of his act, because Eve had fallen and he was not willing that she should be damned alone. Similarly with Michel. He who formerly had sacrificed his love to God, was today, in a sudden reversal, experiencing the frightful temptation to sacrifice God to his love.

"She told me: 'Go and be happy in heaven, leave me to eternal darkness.' Father, that cannot be. Her lot shall never again be separated from mine. If she is to be damned, I wish to be damned. I know that the Church will refuse her religious burial. So I cannot remain in the Church."

Father Athanase put his arm about him and still bending over him sought to instill his own courage into that faltering spirit.

"You are wrong, my friend, my son; you are sick, you are not capable of judging. The Church is not so harsh. Suicide is indeed a great sin in its eyes. But it does not reject those who have committed it in madness, still less those who have had time to repent. Your wife underwent formidable trials. She was misled, she misled us all; she was dominated by a passion which was legitimate in itself but which in time became exaggerated, mad, idolatrous. You were her God! . . . And yet her life was not without generosity. If despair at her disappointed love has lost her for this world, Christ may yet save her for eternity. Remember that her last gesture was toward Him."

At that, a faint light, a far-off flame of hope appeared in Michel's eyes. He listened hungrily to his friend's words.

"Peace be with her," continued Father Athanase.

"Who can know what is taking place there where she is, alone with God, in the total intimacy of this last hour? Aid her with your prayers, as a Christian, as a husband, above all as a priest, for it cannot be that your priesthood is not immensely precious to her at this instant."

Never was a soul about to appear before God supported by more fervent intercession. Overcome by his grief, Father Stéphane repeated over and over the same silent cry: "Have mercy, have pity, I shall expiate for her, I alone am to blame." Father Athanase, more lucid, tense with concentration, fought like an athlete against the forces of evil, bore unwaveringly their last assault, and substituting himself for her who was dying, threw his whole life into the balance before the Supreme Judge. But rich as it was in good works, he counted it for little. The blameless man in him was as nothing beside the priest who had at his disposal an infinite treasure: the blood of Jesus Christ offered by him each morning on the altar. With tranquil, persistent, all-conquering prayer, humble and full of confidence, he petitioned God.

For a long time nothing changed in the room. Life and death fought with equal fury through the body which each claimed, and Michel, clasping it to him, quivered as it quivered. From Father Athanase's lips, like a current of blood from his heart, rose his resolute, unceasing prayer. All three were prisoners of an incommunicable anguish. Their grief, neither increasing nor decreasing, seemed part of eternity. Only the air which entered the half-open window, growing cooler with the night, marked the passage of time.

Then suddenly there was a change. Adélaide's breathing grew feebler, feebler, ceased altogether. Michel's sobs burst out aloud. Father Athanase had risen to his feet. With sovereign dignity, he made a great sign of the cross over the still trembling body. At that last instant when it is said the soul makes its choice, and in the face of eternity accepts or refuses forever the grace which is offered, he repeated once more the formula of absolution, certain that the love which had consumed her in her life was fixed at last upon its true object. As he finished, a deep breath passed the dying woman's lips, then another, weaker, and finally, after an interval, the last.

Although the thoughts of the two priests were above all upon the soul which had just departed, they were tender also toward the poor flesh which it had inhabited and which had been the companion of its long suffering. Piously they rendered her her last honors. When Michel had closed her eyes, and gently brushed her hair, Adélaide took on once more a transitory splendor. Her features which had been contracted, were relaxed; the deep wrinkles which had lined her face were gone. Death before destroying her, clothed her in final loveliness. She emerged from the agony of death more delicate, etherealized, and her beauty took on a character that was at once grave and childlike, uniting the majesty of grief and knowledge with that intangible youth which is of eternity.

She lay, pale and bereft, but one would have said that her body, abandoned by the spirit, was still the bearer of a final revelation. The woman that she had been, long submerged under the turbulent seas of life, appeared now through the calm, limpid waters of death as she truly was. And those who watched beside her, understood her at last. Deceived by her ardor, her nobility, her apparent strength, they had not recognized in her the incurable infirmity of human love. They had been pleased to think of her as free and winged and lucid, when she had been fettered, with that blindfold upon her eyes and that dagger in her heart. But there was Someone who knew her weakness, before whom she was standing now, marked with the wounds of life.

On their knees, the two priests lent her their succor. Michel prayed in the night:

"O, good and loving God, be merciful to her who could not love Thee except through Thy works and who could not penetrate above the world of signs and forms and images.

"She was captive of her senses; she stood in awe of Thy hidden beauty. She sought infinite happiness in Thy creature, but she found it not even in his arms.

She did not understand nor was she understood. Her living body was her cross.

"But Thou, my God, wilt Thou condemn human love, Thou who hast so fashioned man and woman for one another that they must deceive themselves unless they seek each other only in Thee?

"The suffering which they bring one to the other as their only dowry reveals to them, unknowing, the necessity of Thee, leads them, be it only at the end of life, in humility to Thee.

"Thou knowest well that it is for Thee alone that they are yearning, these lovers in their distress, when they hold out their arms for the frail idol that is flesh.

"Thou knowest well that their fault is less great than this void, this emptiness, this desert of deceiving images in which they live.

"But Thou who art Patient and Eternal art waiting for them at their departure from this life, Thou wilt hold out Thine arm to save them. That hour has not yet passed in which Thou didst take upon Thyself their misery with that of all mankind, when Thou camest upon earth to die like them, alone and despised by all whom Thou didst love.

"O let the human heart, which Thou didst carry, go out to this erring one for which we beg forgiveness and which has been pierced by the same lance. In the memory of Thine own suffering grant her surcease from hers for this at least she had in common with Thee: love unrequited."